MW00527082

Mad Scientist Journal: Summer 2018

Edited by Dawn Vogel and
Jeremy Zimmerman

Cover Art and Layout
by Scarlett O'Hairdye

CONTENTS

FICTION

RESOURCES

ABOUT

ACKNOWLEDGMENTS

Many thanks to Patreon backers Simone Cooper, Andrew Cherry, John Nienart, Torrey Podmajersky, Michele Ray, GMark Cole, and Dagmar Baumann!

Visit us at patreon.com/madscientistjournal to lend your support.

LETTER FROM THE GUEST EDITOR

by Dr. Viktor G. Bezummny, PhD,
as provided by Michael Hobbs

What kind of lunatic would submit a scientific paper to the *Mad Scientist Journal*? Could the "mad" truly refer to insanity? Nut jobs seldom consider themselves such. Would not the article, "On the Dielectric Properties of Ectoplasm in a Vacuum: Expansion of ghostly goo under low pressure leads to superconductive phantoms", be submitted to *Science* or *Nature* or *Journal of Materials Science*, instead of this esteemed journal? (And here, I refer you to several articles on the nature of the ectoplasmic reticulum in *Proceedings of Academy of Spectral Studies*, Vol. XXI, London, 1889, for a clear understanding of how *mad* you'd have to be to make a claim of superconductive wraiths - Dr. V.G.B, Phd., ed.) No, self-infected neuroparasitology post-docs are not submitting papers to us on Twitter, one-hundred-forty characters at a time.

Nor would we expect hyperactive, eccentric lab rats to mistake the *Mad Scientist Journal* for the *Madcap Scientist Journal*, which would be an altogether different kind of magazine, one better suited for grocery store check-out lines and dentist's waiting rooms.

No, as Guest Editor, I have chosen articles for this issue of *MSJ* from "mad scientists" who are both brilliant scientists, and angry as hell. Whether they are apoplectic at not being taken seriously, most displeased that their warnings are being ignored, or furious at humanity itself, there are many researchers today whose voices are often lost because the *sublime natures* of their discoveries are overlooked, or because the world is just not ready to accept that there *will be consequences*, or because "… nobody would ever do *that kind of thing*."

For we live now in the kind of peri-apocalyptic world where anger remains as one of the few appropriate emotions, now that hope has been slain, love feels ingenuous, greed is closed to all but the 1%, happiness is fleetingly shallow yet expensive, justice is just ice, and where sadness and sorrow are as mundane as plain oatmeal at a homeless shelter breakfast.

The anger may not be obvious in every paper that appears here. But rest assured that every one of these crazy investigators is plotting the overthrow of *something*. Some just hide it well.

If their results seem hard to swallow, inconceivable, implausible, or unrealistic, one needs suppress the knee jerk reaction of "fake news," and instead examine oneself, rooting out a tendency to jump to quick and convenient (not to mention conventional) conclusions. Reality is more interconnected, non-linear, nuanced, multifaceted, stranger, weirder, sicker, and grosser than we'd like, and it definitely has more leggy, antennae-like bits than we care to imagine.

Remember, too, that irate does not imply irrational, despite a similar string of initial letters. Nor does it indicate irreproducibility. It might be correlated with irascibility, or pertain to iridescence, irradiation, irreverence, or irenics (unlikely), and conceivably could involve iridium, Irish whiskey, or an iridectomy (ewww). But I digress.

In a land of anti-intellectualism as a winning argument *for* anti-intellectualism, SCIENCE MUST BE MAD!

Dr. Viktor G. Bezummny, PhD, is a former Professor of Applied Quantum Intransigence at Universitatea din Ţepeş in Câmpulung, Romania. He grew up in Budapest and is of mixed Polish/Russian ancestry (though rumors of a Romani grandmother won't stay deceased). He has degrees in Extracellular Nucleation from the University of the Witwatersrand, Johannesburg, RSA, and in Exformation and Miscommunications Technology (EMT) from the DolceVita Institute in Vatican City. He also has degrees in Nordic literature and Slavic Agronomic History, both from the Swinburne University of Borneo. In 1999, fearing the predicted repercussions of the then-looming Y2K crisis, he emigrated to the United States, and currently resides in Zillah, WA, where he teaches classical didgeridoo at a local community college when he is not writing articles about science for *Vogue* and *Maxim*.

———

Michael Hobbs won the stock option lottery ("...just what is a stock option?" he asked innocently the first they tried to grant him some) when he was still all but a child, and now he wastes his time very seriously ooogling birds, savoring IPAs and single malt scotches, assiduously attending to the needs of cats, going to readings and concerts with his wife Janka, and generally trying to have fun in the bucket we're all going to hell in. He does not generally consider himself a writer.

ESSAYS

LONELY HEART

Article from the November Issue of The Tri-County News
by Luella Mason, as provided by Kathryn Yelinek

What do you do when you find a beating heart under your lilac bush?

This question confronted Emmeline Harris, 32, of Tomtetown, in April.

"I could tell it was alive," Ms. Emmeline says, pushing aside her kitchen curtains to point out where she made her discovery. "It was shuffling around in the leaves, beating. And it had little legs on the bottom, like in a cartoon. I thought it was a toy at first, but it *felt* real. And it was shivering. Poor thing, all alone in the world."

So what did she do with the heart under her lilac bush?

Ms. Emmeline laughs. "I tucked it in an old cardboard box with a blanket and a hot water bottle. Then I called my sister."

Zora Harris, 34, Fayetteburgh, works at the Tri-County Animal Hospital and is a certified wildlife rehabilitator.

"I'd never gotten a call like that before." She grins at her sister. "I thought Emmeline had sunstroke."

Still, Ms. Zora drove to her sister's house. "Made the trip four minutes faster than usual."

The trip was worth it.

"I couldn't believe my eyes," Ms. Zora says. "It was on the kitchen table, in a box next to the mail. A living, beating human heart."

She quirks her mouth at the memory. "I had to pull a chair out real quick and sit."

Nothing in her fifteen years of working with animals had prepared her for caring for a beating heart.

"I had to be real careful," she says. "Hearts are delicate things."

Luckily, she was able to use an eyedropper to give it saline through its aorta. That worked until she could buy some pig's blood.

"It perked right up after that," Ms. Emmeline says. "I don't know which it craved more—the food or the attention. After each feeding, it would come over, snuggle up to you like a kitten. That was sweet."

"And it loved country music," Ms. Zora says with approval. "One of those songs came on, you know the ones where the guy loses his wife, his truck, and his dog? The heart just started swaying."

Where did it come from? How did it learn to like country music?

"That was the big question," Ms. Emmeline says. "I mean, it's not like we could keep it, right? It wasn't a stray cat that followed me home."

So Ms. Zora picked up the phone. She called the police, who referred her to animal control. Animal control referred her to the police. The hospital sent her to the public library, who referred her to the library at the university. The staff there explained that their science librarian was away at a conference and suggested she contact the biology department. The secretary transferred her to a professor of genetics who happened to be in his office. He dropped the phone when she told him why she was calling.

Fascinating, he said after he retrieved his phone. *May I see it?*

By this time, the heart had gone home with Ms. Zora since Ms. Emmeline's coonhound had shown too much interest in it.

So, on a warm evening in late April, Ms. Zora let Dr. Cletus Hollinger, 36, New Homesdale, into her living room to see her heart.

"It was gorgeous," he gushes. "A perfect human heart, sentient and alive outside of the body. Whoever engineered that was a genius."

And he thought he knew where it had come from.

"The gene hackers have gotten really good," he explains, "and the laws haven't caught up. There's nothing illegal about having a homegrown human heart as a pet."

"But who would do that?" Ms. Zora demands.

A very good question, and one Dr. Cletus can't answer.

"People who grow or keep organs as pets tend to be cliquish," he points out.

"But we had to try," Ms. Zora says. "We made flyers and put ads in the paper and online. The heart was very cooperative and quite photogenic. But the whole thing was sad, you know? Who wants to put up flyers for a lost heart?"

"It was even sadder when no one answered," Dr. Cletus says. "How would you feel if you were a heart that no one claimed?"

"But we wanted it," Ms. Zora quickly adds. "We set up a nice place for it."

In fact, they turned her spare bedroom into a heart playground. The walls are padded to prevent bruising, and there's a wide variety of soft dog and cat toys for it to play with. There's even a little radio that plays country music while Ms. Zora is at work.

"It seems happy," she says, "now that it's found where it belongs."

With that, she takes Dr. Cletus's hand. They share a tender smile.

They've set a date for June. In this case, one lost heart meant that two others were found.

———

Luella Mason's family has lived in Tomtetown since 1689. She shares her two-hundred-year-old farmhouse with her husband, four cats, and a three-legged Pomeranian. After spending twenty-five years as an elementary school teacher, she began her new career as a writer for *The Tri-County News*.

———

Kathryn Yelinek lives in Pennsylvania, where she works as a librarian. She is a graduate of the Odyssey Writing Workshop. Her fiction has appeared in *Daily Science Fiction*, *NewMyths.com*, *Metaphorosis*, and *Deep Magic*, among others. Visit her online at kathrynyelinek.com.

A GIFT FOR MICHAEL

An essay by Doctor Veronica West,
as provided by Maureen Bowden

———

Lucas Vale, the most talented artist to emerge in over a century, was twenty years old and dying. He lay back against his propped-up pillows, eyes sunken in his pale face, his lips tinged blue. "This is for you, Doc," he said, tearing a page from his sketchpad and handing it to me. "It'll be worth a stack of cash when I shuffle off the old mortal coil."

"Thank you," I said, "but don't start giving away your masterpieces just yet. There's still time for me to find you a compatible donor heart, and the transplant team is on standby."

He laughed, a hollow, breathless rattle. "I know you hate to lose a patient, lovely Veronica, but we both know that's a pretty lie. Take the doodle and call it your retirement fund."

The drawing showed a young man hanging by his fingertips from a crumbling cliff face. It was a self-portrait. Like all Lucas's work, it was perfectly executed and strikingly beautiful. It was also disturbing, with a coldness that repulsed me. It lacked heart. I took it back to my office and shoved it underneath a pile of medical journals in my desk's dungeon dimensions, where I wouldn't have to look at it.

I called my secretary. "I don't want to be disturbed, Saffron. Keep the world at bay for an hour or so."

"No prob, Doc," she said.

"And get rid of your chewing gum."

The hospital administrators disapproved of Saffron Kray as my choice of secretary, but she was good at her job and that was all that concerned me. I wasn't deterred by her spiky, blue hair, nose piercing, and the tattoo of a serpent twined around her left wrist, swallowing its own tail. "It's the Worm Ouroboros," she informed me during her job interview.

"Really?" I said. "I wouldn't have slept tonight without knowing that." She was unmoved by irony. I liked her, and I gave her the job.

With my tattooed guard-dog on duty at my door, I left my desk, reclined on the couch in the window recess, and thought about Lucas. His mother had abandoned him when he was six months old, and he was placed in the care system. If a short-term foster carer had not recognised his great talent, he would have had few prospects except a life of poverty and petty crime. He was now the darling of the art world, but his future was about to be snatched from him by a dysfunctional heart. I railed against life's cruelty. "If anyone can provide me with a miracle," I said to the universe in general, "now is the time." I closed my eyes and indulged in the closest I'd ever come to praying.

Saffron knocked on my door and burst in, shattering my reverie. "Sorry to bother you, Doc, but some dude's just barged into Reception and demanded to speak to you about Lucas Vale."

"Oh no, not the press again. I've told them the situation. Without a compatible heart he'll die, and there's sweet Fanny Adams anyone can do about it."

She shook her head. "I don't think he's one of that mob. His name's Max Blackburn. He says you'll remember him."

My head reeled. Of course I remembered him. How could I forget the boy with two hearts?

Twenty years ago, I was a young surgeon with a growing reputation: the cardio-vascular department's rising star. I happened to be on duty the day the post-natal surgical team encountered difficulties while separating conjoined twins.

They called me to assist. Baby Max Blackburn lay on the operating table. A chaotic mass of tissue and bone was attached to his chest cavity, enclosed by the left side of his ribs. Mother Nature had evidently intended it to be his twin, but she'd changed her mind and the foetus stopped developing. The leading surgeon had opened up the ribcage. He expected to face an easy task in separating the healthy baby from the mass, which was incapable of maintaining life.

"Look at this, Doctor West, he said. "We thought the second twin had no vital organs, but we were wrong."

I examined the tiny chest cavity. It contained two beating hearts, connected to each other and to each twin by a branching aorta and vena cava. "Fascinating," I said. "What's the plan?"

He shook his head. "There isn't one. I don't see how I can separate the hearts without endangering the baby. Can you do it?"

"No," I said, "but I can cut off circulation to the undeveloped twin, remove it, and leave the two hearts in the baby's chest." It wasn't as science fiction as it sounded. In transplant operations, the patient's own heart is often left in place as backup, in case the donor heart is rejected. This was a different scenario, but if Max ever had a heart problem, he'd have one to spare.

The operation was a success. I undertook responsibility for the child's follow-up care, and I saw him as an outpatient, every six months for the next seven years.

I remember a conversation I had with him when he was three years old.

"Hello, Max. How are you?"

He shrugged. "Me is okay and Michael is okay, thank you."

"Michael?"

"My brother. He's not got a body, so I take care of his heart."

I glanced at his parents. They smiled indulgently at their son, so I assumed that they had explained the situation to him in those terms. I considered it bizarre, but it was their business, and the child appeared to be comfortable with it.

He developed normally and both hearts remained healthy. After I felt it was safe to discharge him, I hadn't heard from him again until today.

I told Saffron, "Tell Reception to send him up."

Five minutes later, she escorted Max into my office. I motioned him to sit beside me on the couch, and I asked her to bring us coffee.

"How d'ya like it?" she asked him.

"Milk, no sugar," he said.

"Coming up."

As she turned away, he called, "Love the hair." She looked back over her shoulder and winked. He grinned and watched her backside as she sashayed to the door. I felt old.

"Am I right in thinking that you're here because Lucas Vale needs a heart transplant?" I said.

He nodded. "I know you couldn't separate mine and Michael's hearts twenty years ago, but I've done some research, so I know surgery's moved on since then. Can you do it now?

"Yes," I said, "but it would be dangerous. It's very generous of you to offer help to Lucas, but you'd be risking your life."

"I don't see it as a favour to Lucas. I see it as asking him to make a gift of his body to Michael."

"Doesn't it amount to the same thing?"

He shrugged. "Maybe, but I'm looking at it from Michael's perspective."

Saffron interrupted us with a tray of coffee and chocolate macaroons. She placed it on the coffee table in front of us. "The old biddies from the Women's Institute baked the choccy jobbies," she said. "They're well nice."

"You have one," Max said. Before I could comment she took two, and fled.

He drank his coffee and sampled a "well nice" jobbie. "Now can I visit Lucas?" he asked.

"I'll arrange it, but you mustn't build up his hopes too much. I need to do some tests to find out if Michael's heart and Lucas's body are compatible."

"Sure, but don't worry, they will be. Michael told me."

Two days later, I had the test results. They were better than I'd dared hope. I almost ran to Lucas's room to tell him the news. Max was with him. Lucas's voice was barely a whisper, and I could see the vitality fading from his eyes, but the two boys were chatting like old friends.

"The tests are positive," I said. "The heart's a match.

"Of course it is," Lucas said, "and I'll willingly give my body to Michael. Our three lives are in your hands, lovely Veronica."

Before the operation, I spoke to Max's parents. I feared they may disapprove of the risk he was taking, but I was wrong. "We want to thank you, Doctor West," his mother said.

"There's no need, Mrs Blackburn. Max is helping me to save a life, and I'll do all I can to keep him safe."

"There is a need," his father said. "You're giving Michael a chance to live."

Are these people truly deluded? I wondered, or at some level do they understand that the organ Max is donating to Lucas is no more than a biological pump? It's not a person. His brother never actually lived.

Those were the undeniable facts, but when I separated the blood vessels and held Michael's heart in my hands, I felt what I could only describe as a presence, and for a second, I wondered if I were wrong and they were right.

After the operation, Max recovered quickly. He was strong and healthy and suffered no physical ill effects. I was anxious that there might be psychological repercussions following his separation from Michael's heart, but the only consequence that I observed was the bond between him and Lucas, whose convalescence would take longer, due to his months of debilitation. I believe that the hours they spent together every day aided Lucas's return to health.

The other person who aroused Max's interest was Saffron. The day he was discharged from hospital, she said, "Guess who I'm seeing tonight, Doc."

I assumed that "seeing" was a euphemism. "If it's one of my ex-patients who's recovering from major surgery, remember he has no more spare hearts, and don't be too rough with him."

"As if."

My feelings about this development were ambivalent. Max stirred a protective maternal instinct in me, of which I was previously unaware, but a blue-haired aficionado of the Worm Ouroboros may have been what he needed to combat his obsession with Michael.

I visited Lucas. He was sitting in an armchair, sketching, as usual. "Max has gone home," I said.

"I know. He called in to say goodbye."

I pulled up the visitor's armchair and sat beside him. "Will you keep in touch?"

"Of course we will. His family and I are now part of each others' lives."

"I understand that, but I don't understand why they feel that Michael has any real significance."

He put his sketchpad aside and leaned towards me. "You're a doctor, beautiful Veronica. You see reality in scientific terms." He clasped my hand. "I'm an artist. I see it in humanitarian terms, but there doesn't need to be a contradiction. When our perceptions complement each other, they give us a glimpse of the truth."

"You make it sound so simple."

"Maybe that's because it is."

"You're wise beyond your years, beautiful Lucas."

"I don't know about that, Doc, but I know enough, and I've seen how you look at Max. You worry about him, but there's no need. He'll be okay."

"I hope you're right. Have you met Saffron?"

"Yes, she was with him when he came to say goodbye. She brought me a chocolate macaroon."

"He's seeing her tonight."

He laughed. "I know. He's a braver man than I am."

The day Lucas was to be discharged, I arrived at the hospital to find the front entrance besieged by paparazzi pointing cameras at me, and journalists barking ridiculous questions.

"Doctor West, will Lucas's new heart impair his creativity?"

"Is it true a living donor sacrificed his life to save Lucas?"

"Are you playing God, Doctor West?"

I ignored them and made my way straight to Lucas's room. "There's a reception committee waiting outside for you," I said.

"They're wasting their time. I'm making a fast exit out the back." His belongings were scattered in untidy heaps, alongside an empty suitcase, on his bed.

"If you're taking this lot with you it won't be particularly fast. You'll need a couple of trolleys."

"No need. I'm staying with Max and his family for a while. Saffron's arranged for it to be sent to their address."

We heard a knock on the door, and Saffron's voice. "I hope you're decent, Michelangelo. We're coming in."

She and Max burst into the room. Max was carrying two motorbike helmets. He handed one to Lucas.

"What's this?" I said. "You planning The Great Escape?"

"That's about it, Doc. I've parked the bike by the mortuary. It's quiet there. Saffi's leading us out through the emergency fire exit." He turned to Lucas. "Are you ready, Luc?"

"Just give me a minute." He delved through piles of tee shirts, toiletries, and hair gel containers and found his sketchpad. He tore out a page and handed it to me. "For you, beautiful Veronica. It's a companion to the first one I gave you. Thank you for giving me a family, as well as a heart."

Fighting back tears, I hugged him. We said our goodbyes and the escapees headed for the fire exit.

I made a space on the bed, sat down and looked at Lucas's drawing. It depicted three young men roped together, scaling the same cliff face as that shown in the first picture. Two were skilfully drawn likenesses of himself and Max. The third one almost identical to Max, but something indefinable in his demeanour and the expression in his eyes, was all Lucas. The warmth the picture expressed was new to his work. It had heart. He'd signed it "Lucas Michael Vale."

Doctor Veronica West is an eminent cardio-vascular surgeon, recognised as the best in her field. In 2017, she was awarded the OBE for her innovations in heart transplant techniques. Her portrait, by world famous artist Lucas Michael Vale, hangs in London's National Portrait Gallery. It shows an elegant, middle-aged woman, holding a heart in her outstretched palm.

Maureen Bowden is a Liverpudlian living with her musician husband in North Wales. She has had over a hundred stories and poems accepted for publication by paying markets. Silver Pen publishers nominated one of her stories for the 2015 international Pushcart Prize. She also writes song lyrics, mostly comic political satire, set to traditional melodies. Her husband has performed these in Folk clubs throughout England and Wales. She loves her family and friends, Rock 'n' Roll, Shakespeare, and cats.

EPHEMERENE

An essay by Roberta, as provided by Chris Walker

1.

I am holding her close, whispering, when she disappears. The warm pressure of her embrace is gone, and my arms squeeze inward on the sudden emptiness. My words trail away into silence. The faint, familiar scent of her is already fading; I am left with only my yearning.

I wonder how long she will be gone this time. The waiting is what takes the toll. Waiting and not knowing. Of course, it is the same for her when I vanish, but she is better at dealing with it. She has always been the stronger of us.

The clattering of footsteps, like marbles rattling in an urn, echoes in the corridor outside. The fear of it jerks me into stillness, although my heart thrashes in its bone cage. We haven't been gone long enough for our absence to be noticed yet. I think.

We are careful with our stolen moments, because a single mistake could cost us all our future times together. It is strange that we must measure the minutes like a miser coveting his gold coins, here in this place of no time. The days pass and pass but reach no end; we mark them against those who never come back.

I puff out a long breath as the footsteps recede and step away from the cold wall against which I am pressed. I am still in the same room, so I cannot have gone and reappeared myself. All who return do so in the Entrance Hall, although the Great Doors never open. No one has ever seen them do so. Old Maikula claims he knows what lies behind them, but he is mad and we do not believe him.

"Clarissa," I whisper to myself, as if that will make her reappear. It never does.

It is time to go. I need to be at my station soon, or the Overseer will notice and punish me. It seems to enjoy that, as far as we can tell. The opaque mesh that serves as its face never changes, but the groaning noise it makes when it lashes us gets faster and louder.

Carefully, carefully, I pull the door open. The corridor is empty, quiet. I hurry along the drab passages that worm their way through the Castle and make it to my station just seconds before the Overseer appears. A few people sneak glances at me.

"You cut that too close," Rasui hisses at me. "You'll get caught again."

"It's fine," I snap, but I know he's right. Although he can't see the sick feeling in my stomach or the bile that burns my throat, my shaking hands give me away.

The metronomic whirring and popping of the machinery helps to cover our hushed words as we speak, but we keep a wary eye on the bulbous frame of the Overseer as it floats around the long belts and glowing engines. Rasui and I are sorting wotjas and flippits today, easy enough work that doesn't demand full concentration.

"Where's Clarissa?" he mouths.

I shake my head slightly. "Gone again," I whisper.

"Just now?"

I nod.

Rasui grimaces to show his sympathy, but his deep brown eyes are mixed. I'm sure that he is in love with me. Not that he dislikes Clarissa—I don't think anyone does—but I get the feeling that he enjoys these times when she's not with me. If I'm being honest with myself, I've thought about being with him, too. Just once or twice, when a long absence has gotten to me.

I wonder what he feels when I vanish. I think I know.

"After our shift, I'm going to wait for Clarissa in the Entrance Hall," I say. "Will you wait with me?"

Rasui nods. "Of course, Bobby. You know I—"

A loud smashing makes everyone look up, the long rows of workers turning toward the discordance. Maladwa, the young boy who disappears the most, who doesn't speak to anyone except Clarissa, has dropped a fragile wotja on the black floor.

The conveyor belts stop. The Overseer swivels around, gliding toward Maladwa, who cowers for a moment before trying to pick up the glittering glass shards. His frantic actions are in vain.

One of the Overseer's tentacles whips out and coils around the boy. He shouts, and his feet jerk above the floor as he is lifted up. We are all silent, lest we attract its wrath too. The Overseer does something with its tentacle, making it pulse and vibrate with a harsh jangling noise. Maladwa's cries become high-pitched and frenzied.

With deft, fast movements, Old Maikula grabs three wotjas and begins to juggle them. They sparkle in the glare of the lightstones above us as they rise and tumble and fall. The blur of intricate movement is mesmerising.

"Ha ha! Eh?" he beams at the Overseer. The old man nods with foolish, benign eyes, but his hands never stop.

The Overseer whirs, seemingly unsure about this development. Old Maikula inches backward. "Ah, yip yip," he chuckles as Maladwa is dropped to the ground.

The terrified boy scuttles away; the Overseer's full attention is on the spinning, flashing baubles. When Maladwa is out of reach, Old Maikula catches the wotjas, quick as that, and puts them down on the belt with a slight flourish. He grins, showing a mouthful of yellow cracked teeth.

The Overseer's tentacle takes Old Maikula off his feet with the dull smack of metal on flesh. His wrinkled skin splits, scattering fat red drops that arc through the air. Without a sound, the Overseer glides away, tentacles retracting. The belts rumble into life again, and we turn back to them at once.

After a few moments, I look over as Old Maikula struggles to his feet. He resumes his work, the gash across his face streaming blood. He does not wipe it away, although he is careful not to let any of it fall on the wotjas. Maladwa touches Maikula on the arm when the Overseer is not looking, and I see the old man wink at him.

I think about going over to him myself. I must have started to move, because Rasui looks up sharply and takes my wrist. "Bobby, no!"

I sigh and stop. I am still shaking.

Clarissa would have gone.

~

2.

The Entrance Hall echoes as we enter it. It is cold. It does not want us here. The Great Doors reach almost as high as the ceiling, a vaulted space far above us all but lost in the dust and the dark. When we sit on one of the hard benches, Rasui links an arm through mine.

"She'll be fine," he says.

"You don't know that," I reply. "What if she's hurt, or doesn't come back?"

He is silent for a moment, because I am right, then repeats, "She'll be fine."

I squeeze his hand and look out across the worn stone floor, waiting for Clarissa to reappear. No one else in the Castle is here, but I don't blame them. This is always the first sight any of us see when we return from wherever it is that we go to. No one likes to spend any longer in this place than they must. Clarissa and Rasui and I always wait for each other, but that is unusual. Vanishing is like sleeping—oblivion, with the vaguest sense of time having passed, absent any memories or thoughts.

The cold coils around and through us. The stained, ragged clothing we wear is little protection against the chill tendrils. I press myself closer to Rasui, and we share a meagre warmth. He doesn't say anything, but I can feel him smile. I am tired from the fear earlier, drained from the long shift standing up and the racket of the machinery. I can still hear it faintly, but I'm not sure if it's echoing down the long corridors or just inside my head.

"I should've helped Maladwa," I say.

Rasui shakes his head. "You would have been hurt along with him."

"Like Maikula."

"Yes. Like Maikula."

"But—"

"But you're not a crazy old fool like he is," Rasui says.

"Hmm."

"A crazy young fool, maybe."

"Hey!" I cry, giving him a reproachful slap on his chest.

He mock-winces and continues, enunciating each word. "A crazy, young, *beautiful* fool." Rasui's grin is wide, but his eyes—those pretty, dark eyes—are serious.

"That's better," I murmur and rub his chest where I slapped it. His breath catches.

"Bobby—" he whispers, and I hear his longing.

I go still. My other hand is holding his, our arms are entwined. I can no longer feel the cold.

There is a thunderclap from the Great Doors, as if a giant has just slammed two huge boulders together, although they don't move. We leap up, startled, and I almost lose my balance. Clarissa staggers forward as she reappears, then drops to her hands and knees. As the echoing boom dies away, I hear her moaning and whimpering. The wretched sound evokes an ancient, animal response in me, and for a moment I want to shake her until she stops making it. Then I come to my senses and dash to her.

Clarissa turns a purpled, bloody face to me, one eye half swollen shut. "Bobby," she croaks.

I cradle her. "Oh, my love, what's happened to you?"

She swims before my blurred eyes. I hold her and blink until I can see properly. A mass of red-purple bruises covers her stomach where her top rides up, and her ripped leggings are stained with blood across her thighs and crotch. Anguish burns me inside, and fury forces the words through my choking throat. "What have they done? *What have they fucking done?*"

Rasui is by my side now, his mouth set thin and hard. He unscrews the top off a small water bottle, pouring the liquid on to a clean piece of linen. Gently, he wipes the blood away, taking care where strands of her blonde hair stick to her skin.

"You're safe," he soothes, "we're here now. We've got you."

Clarissa's eyes drift across to Rasui's, then back to mine. A smile flickers on her split lips.

"Who did this?" I rasp. "Who did this to you?"

She shivers and looks away.

Rasui stares at me. "She doesn't know. How could she? We never remember where we go, or what happens, or who's there."

He clasps my hand. I know he means to comfort me, but I yank it away.

"Fuck them," I scream.

I am not helping the situation at all. My anger and selfishness is just making things worse, and I curse myself.

"Bobby," mumbles Clarissa. "It's alright. I'm back. I'm alive."

"I'm so sorry," I say to her as my tears make swirling pink tracks down her face.

She understands, as does Rasui. Our helplessness against this unseen and unknowable enemy gnaws at all of us. We don't even know if they—whoever or whatever they are—are just allies of the Wardens, Sentinels, and Overseers in the Castle, or the same as them. We hate them all, regardless.

"Come, let's get out of here and get you to your room," says Rasui.

Clarissa nods, jaw clenched, and we pull her slowly to her feet. I know she's trying to keep silent, but she can't stop herself crying out as she tries to stand upright. Rasui looks at me over her shoulder, a frown pinching his forehead. He's right—it's never been this bad before. Not for the three of us, anyway. And not one person in the Castle knows of a way to stop it.

Clarissa stumbles between us as we hold her up. I can feel her trembling, and it gives a purpose to my rage at last.

I will find a way out of the Castle.

~

3.

"No." Rasui shakes his head fiercely, and even Clarissa voices a protest from where she lies in her bed.

"Roberta," she tells me, "you are *not* going."

"Yes, I am," I retort. "It could be worse next time. What if you're crippled, or ... or never return at all?"

"But the Wardens will catch you," says Rasui. "No one's even gone outside, let alone escaped. You can't go, Bobby."

Their insistence would have stopped me before. I glare at Rasui then Clarissa. "I won't let them hurt you again. I have to do something."

Rasui expels held breath. "You're crazy."

"Not crazy enough to wait around any longer and just watch while awful things happen to the people I love. I'm done with that."

24

Clarissa looks at me. I think my defiance surprises her, almost as much as it does me. "At least wait until I'm well enough to come with you," she pleads.

"No, I've got to do this now," I say. Which is true, as I don't know how long my resolve will last. There is something about this place that sucks the will from you. From me, at least. Clarissa never seems to lack it.

"Then I'll come," says Rasui.

I'm grateful to him, relieved I didn't have to ask.

Clarissa closes her eyes. "Look after her, Rasui," she says.

"You'll be alright here?" I ask her. "We may be gone a while."

"You'd better be back before the next shift starts."

I nod. We should have enough time. I hope.

"We'll find a way. I promise." I lean over and kiss her on her forehead, as her lips are too cracked and painful. She still looks so beautiful. Still stops my heart.

Clarissa manages a smile. "My Bobby," she whispers, touching my cheek.

Rasui whistles from the doorway. "The corridor is clear," he urges.

I want to stay with Clarissa, lie down with her. It would be so easy. I force myself up, though, and walk over to him. Rasui takes my hand as we leave, and I only get a brief last glimpse of her before Rasui pulls the door shut. He does not look back.

The lightstones mounted in the ceiling burn with their cold, unwavering light, casting harsh shadows and highlighting the worry etched on Rasui's face. I must look worse. The doors to other chambers are spaced at regular intervals down the corridor, all closed. No, Old Maikula's is open a crack. I can hear faint singing within his room as we creep past and onward, listening for the tell-tale clatter of a Warden.

I lead us farther down the myriad passageways into areas rarely travelled by the inmates. The thick, ancient stone eats the sound of our feet and presses in. The corridor feels like a throat, constricting and swallowing, as the Castle consumes us little by little. I think of what might lie in its depths, and I shiver. I grip Rasui's hand harder.

"Where are you taking us?" he asks.

"I was sent on an errand once, to a banquet hall," I explain. "There were large windows down one side, but it must have been night-time because all I could see outside was darkness."

"A *banquet* hall?" Rasui says, confused. "Who for?"

I shrug. "I don't know. The table was laden with food that looked and smelled freshly-cooked, but there was no one there, and every surface was covered with thick dust."

"Ah, real food sounds good. Better than that disgusting paste we get."

"Don't even think about it. We're here to find a way out, not for you to fill that scrawny belly of yours."

He sighs, and pats his stomach. "Maybe the next time I vanish, I'll get a good meal."

I almost smile at his feigned little-boy-lost look and finally do when he grins at me.

"Come on," I say, poking him, "I think it's somewhere around here."

~

The surroundings have a touch of forgotten opulence, as if they were magnificent but have faded with long decades. Not tarnished or grimy, more that they are colourless and somehow dimmed, caught in the act of slow disappearance into distant memory.

A faint glow spills from a gap in the wall up ahead.

"Is this it?" asks Rasui.

"I don't think so," I reply, "I don't remember this passage. We must have come from a different direction."

I peer round the archway and into an almost spherical chamber, stopping at the sight. Rasui bumps into me.

"Who is that?" he says.

A man stands upon a raised platform in the middle of the room. No, not standing, I realise. He is floating just above it. A column of pale, steady light surrounds him, the only illumination in here. His eyes are closed, and he hangs there without moving.

A large round clock, splendid with ornate decorations, hangs above him on the otherwise blank wall. I see the longest hand ticking round, nibbling away at the seconds, but it makes no sound.

"I've never seen him before," whispers Rasui.

I look more closely at the suspended figure. He wears long dark robes patterned with complex whorls of silver thread—rich clothes once, but they look tattered now. Although he is an older man, his

26

face is lined and creased beyond his apparent years, telling of some deep misery.

When I glance up at the clock, its hands have changed their positions, though only a minute has passed. I turn to Rasui and nudge him, pointing at the clock. When I look back, it shows yet another time.

"Did you see—" I begin.

A familiar clacking and rattling in the distance spikes fear into us.

Rasui grabs my arm. "Which way?" he asks.

"But what about him?"

"No time."

I rack my memory. "It's this way."

We sprint down the corridor, rounding a corner to see a large, metal-bound wooden door ahead.

"There!" I say.

We burst through it, spilling into the banquet hall. It is different now. The huge table is barren, and the room is spotless, with no trace of the smothering dust that I witnessed before. I have to stop myself shouting when I see the two seated figures—a man and a woman at either end, dressed in finery, staring at each other. If they see us, as they must, we are finished.

But they don't move. Rasui does, striding up to the woman while I remain as motionless as them. He waves a hand in front of her, and then touches her cheek.

"Mannequins, I think—."

His tone is one of relief, although his eyes narrow in puzzlement.

"It's getting closer," I hiss at him.

One of the larger Wardens, by the sound of it. This is bad. Rasui runs to the door and peeks out as I hurry to the large windows. They are elegant and well-crafted, set just above my head in the hard grey walls. It must be night outside again, as I can see only a dulled image of the banquet hall reflected in the spotless panes. I jump and grab the windowsill, scrabbling to pull myself up.

"Shit!" Rasui's hoarse whisper snaps my head around as he ducks into the room. "It's coming this way."

I look over the room frantically, but there's just the one door. No other exits, except for the windows. I struggle with the thick latch at the base of this one as my panicked face stares back at me.

The utter darkness out there is impenetrable, and I can't see any lights or clues as to what lies beyond. Maybe a drop to certain death; I realise I don't even know how high up we are. Stupid. What had I been thinking?

My fingers refuse to work, and I curse and fumble with the simple task. We aren't going to make it.

"Rasui, get up here!" I call, wondering what's taking him so long.

Silence. I look round again. He's standing in the doorway, lost in thought. The Warden's racket is growing louder.

"I'll lead it away," he says after a moment.

"*No!*" I beg. "This way."

"Too risky." Rasui gazes at me. "Bobby, I—"

And then he vanishes. Not down the corridor. He's just gone. For a moment I'm frozen, then something in me breaks, and I jerk the window up.

Nothingness.

There is nothing outside.

The blackness isn't night, it's just a void. My mind recoils and spins near hysteria, sliding away each time I look into that null space. I can't even see the anticipated masonry of the Castle when I look down, and I begin to feel faint.

I am nowhere. *We* are nowhere.

The clamour of the Warden fills the air with terrifying closeness. I'm trapped. What final choice do I make about how I meet my end?

Except ...

I jump down and run to the female mannequin, yanking her out of the chair. I am surprised at how heavy she—it—is, but a desperate strength takes over. I heave it out of the window, which I then slam shut, expecting the Warden's clapperclaws in me at any second. I throw myself into the empty chair and force myself to sit motionless.

The harsh jangling enters the room. My back is not quite to the door, but I don't dare move even my eyes to look. My head whirls, and my heart gibbers like a mad beast as I hold my breath. A thunderous drumming fills my ears. I strain to keep my body immobile, fighting the urge to run, focusing every ounce of will I can to this unnatural inaction. It is the one chance I have.

The Warden sounds like a rain of metal skulls filling a steel coffin as it scuttles closer; it is right behind me. Perhaps the void would have been better after all.

I start to ready myself, even knowing as I do so that it is futile, when it moves off. A trick? But no, it is gone from the room, carrying its turmoil away down the passage. And I sit there, drained, unable to move where a moment ago I thought I wouldn't manage to hold still. I don't even have the energy to weep.

Then footsteps, before I can react. I do look this time and see Old Maikula striding into the room. He halts, and his face is solemn as he regards me. Then it splits into a wide smile.

"That was close, eh? Ha ha!" he beams.

~

4.

"That's ridiculous!" I scoff. "I don't believe you."

But Maikula just gazes at me, all traces of the foolish old man gone. Clarissa regards him, thinking, silent. A cold weight settles in my stomach.

After the hasty retreat from the banquet hall, we are again in Clarissa's room, which is a risk in itself. My chamber is some distance away, and the chance of my being found missing from it increases with each passing minute. Right now, I don't care.

"Haven't you wondered why you never *dream*?" asks Maikula.

I start to answer, then stop as the word stirs a memory, faint and sluggish, a slow creature of hidden deeps. I try to grasp it, but it's as elusive as a shadow.

"You've seen him already, I gather," says Maikula, "the one who has imprisoned us here, forever apart from the world. The one who does not let us go onward to our rest."

"That man who was floating in the light?"

"Indeed."

"But he seemed ... he wasn't dead, but I'm sure he was more than just sleeping," I say. "Why can't we escape?"

"I shall start at the beginning, then," says Maikula, "for after all, that's what they are for.

"There was a boy who lived in a great city by the sea. He had, for a time, a comfortable and exciting life as the sole child of parents gifted in the arcane arts. They doted on him and took him with them wherever they went. He learned many things—of people, of creatures, of magic, of knowledge ... and of power. As I said, his life was exciting. What few friends he had were certainly envious.

"But one day there was a terrible accident, and his mother and father were killed. He had their castle and wealth but was left alone, without their love. He began to see them in his dreams, and, as the boy grew, he became obsessed with sleeping so that he could still be with his parents. But their memory faded with time; he was young when they died, and the mind plays tricks with our recollections."

"The poor boy," says Clarissa. "He lost them completely in the end."

"Yes, he did." Maikula bows his head, then continues. "After many years, he became a sorcerer himself—master of the elements, of people, of things of metal and stone and wood—and, after a fashion, of death itself. He vowed that he would help others who suffered as he had, that he would try to bring some measure of comfort to them.

"However, his obsession held him in thrall. It was a slow and insidious poison that ate at him, perverting his noble intentions. He devised a method where, at the moment of their death, he could prevent the spirits of people from passing into eternal oblivion, and send them instead into the dreams of others as he chose."

"But that's horrible," I say.

Maikula voice is sad. "He thought he was doing good, you see. He couldn't—or wouldn't—accept the pain he was causing, or that his actions were abhorrent. When the other sorcerers in the city finally learned of his atrocities, they denounced him. He was given the title 'Slumber-Mage' in mockery and contempt of what he had become. The people, outraged, rose up and tried to execute him. He fled to this realm, taking the Castle with him."

"And here we are," I say.

"Yes. Forevermore."

"How do you know all this?" asks Clarissa.

"I was his apprentice." Maikula's mouth twists. "When I found out what he was doing, I tried to get word to the others. But, before I could, he discovered my betrayal and ... well. You can guess."

"I'm sorry," I say.

30

"It was very long ago," he replies, shrugging.

"So all we are now are just figments in other peoples' dreams," states Clarissa. She has accepted it.

"You've seen outside," says Maikula to me. "You know. Even if it's hard to admit it to yourself."

And I know the truth of it. I think I always did, in a way.

"But what is he doing now?" I ask. "Can we fight him?"

Maikula sighs. "No. His body is here and is protected, but *he*— that is, his spirit—isn't inside."

"So where has he gone?"

"I don't know. It's been many years, and he has never returned. Perhaps he still searches for his parents." Maikula sighs. "I do know that after he left, everything began gradually turning to chaos. The arcane engines and mechanisms that he built to run this place are falling into disrepair, so are malfunctioning. We are being sent to dreamscapes that we were never meant to go to, into the minds of people—dreadful people—that we were never meant to be part of. And what happens to us there, what they do to us, has a real effect."

Clarissa turns pale. "Can't we fix things?"

Maikula shakes his head. "Even the Machinists don't seem to be able to stop the decline."

I stare at Maikula. "Then there's nothing we can do."

He spreads his hands. "I'm sorry."

Clarissa looks at up me. "You've stayed too long here, Bobby," she urges. "You have to get to your room."

"Yes!" says Maikula. "Go!"

"But Rasui—I'm going to be on shift. I won't be able to wait for him," I say.

Clarissa starts to rise from the bed, and I press her back down. "No," I tell her, "you need to rest."

"I'll wait for your friend," offers Maikula. "Roberta is right. You should regain your strength. Things are going to get worse."

"Thank you," I say.

I kiss Clarissa in a lingering goodbye, reassuring myself that I can feel her warmth and softness, that she is still real for me, and I for her. Then I leave, slipping through the winding warren of passages that lead to my room. I lie there, spent and dazed, my thoughts as formless as the void outside, as Maikula's words entwine me like blacksteel chains and pull me down into a dreamless sleep.

~

5.

I smash my fists in useless rage on the Great Doors. "Give him back to me, you bastards!" I howl.

The sound is flat and dulled, swallowed by whatever lies on the other side of them. Clarissa pulls me to her, holding me, wiping away the tears that fall in hot streaks down my cheeks. We hug each other for long moments before Maikula speaks.

"I'm very sorry. Given the number of days that have passed since he vanished, it's ... no. Rasui is never going to return. I'm sorry."

I grit my teeth to stop from screaming.

"Where is he? Is he dead?" asks Clarissa.

"Mmm," Maikula frowns. "Snared in a dream-catcher, perhaps. Or maybe he's been trapped inside a damaged mind or, more likely, one that cannot wake up. Not until the host dies will he die himself."

"And that would be a blessing," says Clarissa. I feel her tears on my face, mingling with my own.

"Yes." Maikula nods once.

The thought of poor Rasui trapped and beyond escape crushes my heart, tearing a plea from my lips. "Let him die. Please."

That the same could happen to Clarissa is too much to bear. I break her embrace and grab Maikula by his shoulders.

"I can't go on," I shout at him. "Not like this. Not wondering each time Clarissa vanishes if that's the last time I've seen her. There must be *something* we can do."

For an old man, he feels strong in my grasp. But then, he wasn't the mad fool he pretended to be, either.

"Perhaps," he says at last. He looks at me, his eyes flicking between mine. "Do you love Clarissa?"

"Yes. Her, always. Yes."

Maikula gives a slight smile, although his eyes don't change. "I know. As long as you know it, too."

He returns me to Clarissa's side and clasps his hands together.

"The things we make and sort during our busywork—the

wotjas and flippits and whojams—do you know what they are?"

"Given what you've told us, I think they're dream entities," guesses Clarissa.

"Ha! Good!" Maikula beams. "This one's a keeper," he says to me, winking. "Yes. These are mutable, adaptable things. A genius creation of the Slumber-Mage, I have to admit. They get sent into people's dreams and turn into whatever they need to be, shaped by the subconscious thoughts and desires of the host. Genius!"

"How will they help us?" I ask.

"Those can't," he says, "but there is another type that you won't have seen—a klarojem. Rare. Stored in a special workshop. They allow the host to have lucid dreams, although I believe the Slumber-Mage had other aims in mind when he created them. But for us? Well, they let *us* dream."

I can tell that Clarissa has thought of something by the way she gives a soft gasp. I'm lost, though. "So what do we do with them? And why don't *you* use one to escape, then?"

Maikula nods. "I won't use a klarojem because I have nowhere to go. Precious few here, if any, do. But you and Clarissa—you have each other."

The meaning of his words flashes in me like fire, and I throw my arms around Maikula and then Clarissa. I can't laugh, not with Rasui gone. Any happiness is consumed by his loss. But now I have hope.

~

6.

The Overseer's grapnel smashes into the side of the workbench where my head was an instant ago. I scramble to seize the end of its tentacle before it retracts and hang on with both hands. It jerks me off balance and on to the hard floor, skinning my knees and elbows.

Maikula jabbers at it, throwing a couple of whojams at its head with remarkable aim. The heavy objects knock the gleaming dome so that it tilts to one side.

"Yip yip," he chortles, as the Overseer turns to him.

Another whojam finds its mark, denting its mesh face with a satisfying impact. It emits a wheezing noise and sinks to the floor. Clarissa dashes out from her hiding place, stone block held high in both hands. The back of the Overseer's head is toward her, its exposed innards glinting and whirring.

As she throws the block, another tentacle lashes blindly at her. It catches her under her upraised arms; there is a sickening crack as her ribs break. She cries out in pain and collapses. The stone mass clips its target before caroming off and splitting on the floor.

The tentacle I'm holding goes limp, so I yank it under and around the sturdy metal workbench just before it returns to life. I brace my feet against a support, pulling with all my strength. The tentacle vibrates and a searing pain shoots up my hands, coursing through my body. I yell with the effort and agony of it, but do not let go.

Another whojam finds its mark, distracting the Overseer again, but they won't be enough to finish it on their own.

"Hammer!" cries Maikula, pointing at a row of tools hung on the wall near Clarissa.

She scrambles to her feet, clutching her side and moaning, but manages to duck under the machine's now clumsier attacks to grab the hammer from its hook. It is big and needs both her hands to wield. As she staggers toward the Overseer, I wrench its tentacle once more, just enough to tip it forward a little.

The hammer swings up, up, holds at the top of its terrible arc, then smashes down into the jittering intricacies that drive the inhuman mechanism. The Overseer's howls mingle with Clarissa's as she swings the hammer over and over.

And then it is finished.

I rush to catch her as she starts to crumple. We stink of metal and sweat, of anger and torment and animal panic. We are alive.

Maikula limps over, bleeding from the long gash in his leg, and looks down at the wrecked contraption. It twitches and rattles at our feet, erratic, slowing.

"That went better than I expected," he grimaces, "but we need to move quickly. There'll be more on their way. Sentinels, too. Come with me."

He turns and hobbles over to a panel at the back of the workshop. He slides it up, revealing a compartment containing several blue-silver stars the size of his thumb. They sparkle with a light of their own. With great care, he takes two and hands one each to me and Clarissa. They feel so cold; I almost drop mine in surprise.

"Klarojems. Eat them," he says.

"That's it?" Clarissa asks.

"That's it. You'll fall asleep almost immediately."

"But what about you?" I say. "What will you do?"

"Ah, don't worry about me, girl," he says. "Old Maikula will be just fine. Ha ha!"

The lined face crinkles as he gives me a last wink, eyes bright.

I take Clarissa's hand in mine, and we smile at each other. I think of all those stolen moments leading to this point. However many we had, they were never enough. She was my refuge, I her light. Now we are something more.

Together, we swallow the dreamstones and vanish into each other's tomorrows.

Roberta's past remains unknown to her, despite the aching hours she has spent trying to remember where she came from. Hours ... or days, or years? She is not sure, for these concepts don't feel appropriate. Her wife, Clarissa, does not worry about such things and laughingly reminds her that the present moment is all they need. On occasion, the image of an old man flashes in Roberta's mind; more than a dream and less than a memory. She knows, without understanding how, that he is from a place unimaginably far away, just on the other side of yesterday.

Chris Walker is a professional byte-wrangler and sometime astrodynamicist. He enjoys writing stories of other worlds and days that might be. Or will been going to had being, if it wasn't for that pesky malfunctioning Time Drive. Yes, the one he swears he will read the manual for at some point. Chris lives in the UK and loves the liquid phase of what you humans call coffee.

GENEMECH ANNOUNCES BIO-SECURITY INCIDENT AND CONFIRMS RELEASE OF GIANT DEATH BEES

A press release authorised by Dr. Mackenzie Cooper, Chief
Science Officer and Co-Founder Genemech,
as provided by Paul Alex Gray

FOR IMMEDIATE RELEASE

VENUS SPRINGS, NEVADA, October 12t[h], 2019
/PRWorldWire

Genemech (NYSE: GMNX) today announced a bio-security incident originating in the company's WN45 facility. WN45 is a classified advanced manufacturing site developing a range of products and technologies used by governments and industry around the world.

Our initial findings confirm that a premeditated act of sabotage has been carried out by a rogue scientist, Dr. Maximilian Benetton. Dr. Benetton led Genemech's Genetically Enhanced Insecta Applied Research Lab (GEIARL), which uses Clustered-Regularly-Interspaced Short Palindromic Repeat (CRISPR) augmentation techniques to implant custom RNA code into genetic material. In a manifesto published online, *Give me control of Genemech or my Giant Death Bees shall paint the skies with blood,* Dr. Benetton advised that a new strain of genetically modified bees have been released, using enlarged Genemech Batch 2492M GMBee©™ honeybees enhanced with venom from the taipan, a highly venomous snake endemic to Australasia.

At this time, there have been no reports of Giant Death Bee attacks.

Upon confirming the sabotage, Genemech immediately froze Dr. Benetton's access to the company's control systems and notified global authorities. Our analysis indicates that approximately 3.4 million bees were created, with 2.9 million passing larval stage. Company logs show that the bees were secretly removed from the facility on October 9th by Dr. Benetton, who has not been seen since. The location of the bees is currently unknown, although our security team analysed logs that suggest Dr. Benetton may be on Isla Salvador, an uninhabited volcanic island in the South Pacific.

"This is a disappointing event for Genemech, a technology company striving to deliver the best outcomes for our planet. I apologize to our customers, investors and the worldwide community for the inconvenience this may cause," said Chief Science Officer and Co-Founder Mackenzie L. Cooper. "We are currently considering a number of options to neutralise the threat."

Genemech confirms that GEIARL animals can have latent behavioural and biological capabilities that can only be initiated by use of certain proprietary chemical compounds. It is feasible that Dr. Benetton can activate "breed mode" and "attack mode" commands, similar to our military product lines. This may be achieved through audio signals, olfactory cues, or subtle use of light to activate the chemical compounds.

Genemech has published helpful information on our website to assist citizens of planet Earth determine any risks they may face and provide helpful information on how to respond in the event of an attack. We recommend downloading our app (available from iTunes and Google Play), which will provide warnings if the bees are activated and have been detected in your area. Fundamentally, Genemech recommends avoiding fields and flowers and fleeing any bees that you may encounter. You should remain indoors as much as possible until we confirm the threat has been neutralised. Genemech is offering a discount on our Bee, Wasp, and Scorpion survival kits comprising Bio-Chem insect repellant and double headed fly-swatters. (Visit our site or app to learn more and order.)

Genemech is exploring several workable solutions, including, but not limited to, offering Dr. Benetton a new corner office on the eleventh floor, the immediate release of enhanced T94 "Typhoon" Japanese Hornets, which will seek out and destroy all bees on Earth, or the use of a small-scale tactical nuclear strike on Isla Salvador.

Dr. Cooper said "I've instructed my entire team to give this issue their full attention. Building a bio-secure future is what drives Genemech each and every day, and we've made significant investments in this space. We recognize we must address this threat, but also strive to be a better company and global citizen. For now, stay inside and try to relax."

About Genemech

Genemech is a global genetic-engineering company that develops bio-enhanced insects, fish, reptiles, and mammals to help governments, industry, and militaries to achieve more with less. Our products include GMBee©™, the world's first disease and pesticide resistant bee, and TigerBear-3000™, used by military and police forces worldwide for riot control, general policing, and urban combat.

Founded in 2007 by renowned scientists Dr. Mackenzie L Cooper and Dr. Haruko Takahashi, Genemech is headquartered in Venus Springs, Nevada, and operates or has research facilities in 17 countries in North America, EMEA, and Asia. Its common stock is traded on the New York Stock Exchange under the symbol GMNX.

Twice nominated for the Nobel Prize, Dr. Mackenzie L. Cooper is the world's leading scientist in genetic augmentation. After completing her second PhD at the age of twenty-three, Dr. Cooper was inspired by the power of nature to develop means to expedite evolution. In 2006, she successfully manufactured a snake-bird hybrid and in 2007, she established Genemech with her co-founder, Dr. Haruko Takahashi. Dr. Cooper is an advocate for using science to make bold changes to improve the world we live in. Outside of work, Dr. Cooper enjoys extreme running, and she has twice won the ultra-distance desert marathon.

Paul Alex Gray enjoys writing linear and interactive fiction that cuts a jagged line to a magical real world. His work has been published in *Nature Futures*, *McSweeney's*, *Empyreome*, and others. Paul grew up by the beaches of

Australia, then traveled the world and now lives in Canada with his wife and two children. Over the years, Paul has been a startup founder, game designer, and mentor to technology entrepreneurs. Chat with him on Twitter @paulalexgray or visit www.paulalexgray.com

A RECORD OF ANDROID M14DA3-Y2015'S LAST WEEK IN HEADQUARTERS

As told by Employee ID 3583002, transcribed by Teo Yi Han

T minus four days

All the way to work I debated with myself and changed my mind about once approximately every five minutes:

Ask her for a photo together

Don't do something so ridiculous, please

What do you have to lose at this stage

She is going to stare at me, uncomprehendingly, and it is going to make me feel bad that I've done something out of convention that she has not been programmed to respond to, that my behavior is out of human average again.

I tossed the options in my mind one last time; they landed, heads up.

Don't care, I thought, *don't care what she thinks, don't care.*

Even if she thought me weird, I would still have my photo.

She wasn't at her usual place when I walked into our shared cubicle. I pulled out my phone and saw that the automatic message notification had been sent much earlier, in the midst of all the flip-flopping of decisions: one of her parts had malfunctioned, and she had been sent back for maintenance.

I didn't even need to fret over it after all.

Later that morning, I was in the toilet cubicle, staring at the back of the door blankly. Someone was crying softly two cubicles down. Occasional soft sob and hiccup. Not even trying to hide. When I cry in the toilet at work, no sound is allowed to escape from my throat. I stayed still and silent so as not to disturb. I decided if I walked out and saw the person I would ask her, *Are you okay?* I would offer a hug.

I wondered if it was a colleague I knew.

I waited. The other person waited too. For me to leave.

So I did. I didn't get to see who she was.

~

She never cried. Not at work, not ever. I was pretty sure they did not build that function in her. She had seen me cry. Twice. She did not know I was crying because of her. The first time she saw me cry, she silently walked away, got a piece of tissue, placed it on my table, and then resumed working wordlessly.

It must be good to never cry. To never be plagued by the need to cry. To not have this boundless well of unbidden salt water.

~

T minus three days

There was one last lunch with the whole team. Someone was talking to fill the silence. She wasn't talking much, but she was listening intently, storing everything away, never to be forgotten. She wasn't eating, she didn't have to, but she was accompanying us.

When she first joined our department, she had refused to go for lunch with us. "I do not require biological sustenance for survival," she had informed us factually. Curtly and coldly, I had thought back then, annoyed. Factually and accurately, I understood later. Then she had ignored us and continued working, while we exchanged looks as we walked away, beings that did require biological sustenance to survive, and breaks to recharge.

There she was, sitting with us, partaking in lunchtime rituals even if she did not see the point of that, listening to our conversations, occasionally even asking questions, not to gain knowledge, but merely to be social.

I cut up the sausage into half-inch slices. Tried to make sure the slices were of the same width, but they were not. Some were thicker and some thinner. Gave up. Dismantled the burrito. Unrolled it carefully. Picked out each cube of peppers one by one. Separated the sliced mushrooms from the scrambled eggs. Cut up the now flat piece of tortilla. Piled a slice of mushroom, a suitable amount of scrambled egg, some cheese onto each piece of tortilla. Topped it off with an uneven slice of sausage. Tried to put the whole thing into my mouth all at once.

Focused on cutting up food, so I didn't stare at her, sitting next to me, while I left an overly generous amount of space between us, didn't think about how this was the last time she would be sitting next to me at a lunch table. Kept piling neat piles of food into my mouth, so I didn't have to talk, so the things that couldn't be said, would remain unsaid.

When Jasmine left, we held one last team lunch for her too.

Jasmine, who'd taught me everything about the place.

Jasmine, who always had a ready ear to listen to complaints about work, supervisors, other co-workers.

Jasmine, who had a response for every topic.

Jasmine, who partook in numerous in-jokes.

Jasmine, who was not just a work friend, who went out for dinners and weekend brunches too, when she didn't have to.

Jasmine, who dug the trenches beside me day in and day out and taught me how to look out for the warning signs and friendly fire and how to hide and saved me from an occasional bomb or two.

Jasmine, who told me, right before she left, "You have to get out of here too, okay. This is no place to stay for long. You must find a way out."

Then Jasmine was gone.

Soon after, they brought her in to replace Jasmine.

(I will admit, this is a revision of history. See, I thought of her as an it, back then.)

I couldn't stop staring at it when they first brought it in. It looked so much like a real human. Robotics technology was amazing. More productive than any human. No emotions. No need to eat or sleep. Smarter than any human. Brain a processor. Makes no mistakes. Works at twice the speed of an average human.

It would soon outdo me in everything it did.

But all I wanted was a friend. Someone who would offer a hug when things were going terribly at work. Someone who would laugh at the absurdities with me. Not processors and coding that only looked human, no matter how startling the resemblance.

~

T minus two days

"An android, and a female one no less!" Amy had teased me when she first found out.

Why not, I had thought.

~

She swiveled her chair over to my desk in the afternoon, and she briefed me, one last time, on her work that I would take over after she was gone.

She was close. Very close. She rested her arm on the armrest of my chair. She was so close, I could almost feel her heat, if I imagined there was any heat radiating from her. Maybe the heat of her processor overheating. Physical distance didn't mean anything to her. Warmth, skin, blood, the gap between us I felt every inch of acutely didn't mean anything to her. Things that distracted didn't mean anything to her. Her focus was pure work, she was smooth efficiency sharpened to a fine tip.

There was so much to memorize. There was too much to memorize. The way they had her hair tied back in a high ponytail. The way her eyes could crinkle when she simulated laughing, head fully thrown back. The way she gestured when she talked, amazingly human-like. The motion of her elegant, slender, well-designed fingers. The almost gleam in her eyes when she talked about something she was almost passionate about. (Do androids have passion, I wondered. Is the dancing spark in her eyes a trick of the light, the blinking lights of a functioning machine, or just the delusion of my mind?) The almost amused look on her face when I attempted to make a joke. The way she looked over, just to catch my eye, in silent agreement. The way she remembered everything. Her analysis and undefeatable ability to break everything down, to unearth every possible option, to calculate everything to an inch of its life. The streams of information coming from her I could never hope to fully remember.

I didn't have her memory drive, after all.

Even as I was gazing at her, these things were all falling away from me like sand, impossible to grasp at, taunting me over what I would soon be bereft of.

They said you're not supposed to develop any feelings for androids. Androids were capable of a great deal in the workplace,

44

far exceeding human capabilities. They were, however, incapable of returning any human feelings. This was their advantage here.

These were the things that ran laps in my brain, that I kept carefully hidden away, as she was detailing her work processes to me, so close I could almost touch her. Things that I knew she did not comprehend, that burned all the way down in me. She rattled off facts, figures, grabbed my pen and scribbled on sheets of paper, while I thought about the shape of her calves then beat myself up for objectifying her, and asked myself if it was worse if she had been a real human female, or that she was not.

Her brain did somersaults around me, and all I could do was watch from my seat, mouth agape, give up any hope of trying to keep up, and merely settle for clapping at the display like a trained seal.

During the days, basking in her presence, her steady gaze, the familiar, comforting, constant stream of the rapid but smooth tapping at her keyboard, the soundtrack of office life—the seconds run too fast, days and universes are lost in conversations with her, in the tenor of her voice.

During the nights, where her absence turns everything to abyss, the moments turn into sludge, keep eyelids open, stop time, space, narrow everything down to one recurring thought, drill through skull, squishy brain—the seconds freeze, shatter, sending shards down bloodstreams.

Every moment with her is a stolen moment, that I hoarded greedily, that would never be sufficient no matter how many I collected.

~

T minus one day

It was easy to retreat to another familiar train of thought, that I should take time off from work for her last day. I had thought about it months ago when it was still feasible, to weeks ago while the window of opportunity was slowly shutting down, and at that point still I thought of applying for medical leave the next day. Tell the doctor, *I'm sick to my stomach. I want to throw up.*

And it would've been true.

"Don't," Amy replied. "You have to be there. Till the bitter end. You can't run away. You have to see it through. Or you'll regret it in the future."

"Why," I asked, even though I knew well why, even though I knew my feet will be rooted.

"Closure," Amy said simply.

I knew Amy was right. I knew it would also feel amazingly like taking a sharp knife and carving grooves into my arm and watching the blood drip.

I could still fantasize about going to the doctor's the next day though, spilling woes of a lack of wellness. Not turning up. Not being there for the last day. Not watching everything spin out of control. Not watching the car crash happen to me, in slow-motion, three hundred and sixty degrees angles, shot from above, shot from the front, shot from the sides.

She was away at one last meeting so I used the opportunity to commit her desk to memory. Her desk had always been devoid of personal effects. Not necessary for work. I could see why they would want to introduce her and others like her into the workplace. If someday humans like me were obsolete and replaced by the likes of her, it would be because we were defeated by our useless, cumbersome emotions.

I fought the urge to take a photo of her desk. It was almost empty save for the necessities anyway, and soon it would be completely empty.

Void, like the void she would soon crater in my heart, like the cracks that had started forming when they announced they would soon transfer her to another branch for them to test her capabilities in a different area, for her to build up her repository and storage of information.

She had smiled and agreed pleasantly that she was looking forward to going to a different office and learning new things and picking up new skills.

I looked into her eyes and they were clear, and there was nothing, absolutely nothing behind them, not a flicker of emotion, not a hint of feeling, nothing.

At that moment, it became startlingly clear that despite all our pleasant interactions, all the shared battles, all the camaraderie, all these time, I meant nothing to her. She would not miss me. She would not be sad. She had just been recording everything, without affect. She would leave completely unaffected.

That was how she had been built, had been programmed, after all. The fact evoked envy. I wished I could be programmed that way too.

Not the bleeding mess that took up residence in my ribcage, spread into my brain through the folds, rendered my brain useless.

I turned back to stare at her sparse desk. The smooth planes of wood, the coils of black wires. When they removed her, they were going to remove everything.

Better get used to it. This was going to become the new normal.

But she was still going to haunt my dreams and waking hours.

Do androids dream of electric sheep? Do humans dream of androids? What was the point? Androids would never dream of humans in turn.

~

I managed to get my photo with her in the end. Oh, how ludicrous it all was. Trying to capture a snapshot, the sentimentality of the moment. To an android, all moments were devoid of significance. All moments merely led to the next, and the next, and the next, in a logical sequence of programmed commands, to continue into infinity if unobstructed.

I had waited till a lull between her rapid bursts of elegant typing. I steeled myself. I posed the question to her.

She looked at me questioningly.

"Here? Now? In the office?"

Something wilted inside of me. I tried to keep my voice steady. "Yes. Here. And now."

She gave me the look that told me I've again done something not in her programming, but she acquiesced in the end.

She moved stiffly next to me and pasted on a smile accommodatingly. I fumbled with the camera on my phone, and took three tries to get it right, growing increasingly nervous.

When I finally got the photo I told her, *thank you*. She looked at me like she didn't get it, but she didn't say anything else as she went straight back to her work, beautiful elegant fingers flying over her keyboard again as though she never paused.

Later when I looked at the photo, I saw that she moved so close to me, we were actually touching. She had closed the physical gap between us completely, only the physical gap.

At the end of that day, I said goodbye to her as I walked past her desk when I left, as I've done every evening for the past two years.

"Goodbye," she intoned automatically, not looking up, gazing intently at her computer screen, processor a million miles away, and probably in a million different directions simultaneously too.

I knew to her, I had been stored away, another insignificant data point out of a million others, never to be retrieved again.

~

T minus zero

<End of Recording>

Employee ID 3583002 has learned not to fall in love with company made-to-order androids and will spend her spare time on dating sites looking for human males or females to date instead. She has made great strides towards reducing the incidences of alternatively crying and cursing at any complex piece of technology. Please send any potential dating partners (HUMANS ONLY!) her way.

Teo Yi Han is a Singaporean policy analyst with a degree in psychology who struggles with policy writing by day and narrative writing by night. One of her stories won 1st prize in the Singapore 2015 Golden Point Award short story category, and others have been published in Southeast Asian anthologies such as *FLESH: A Southeast Asian Urban Anthology* and *This Is How You Walk On The Moon: An Anthology Of Anti-Realist Fiction*.

GRANDMA VISITS

An essay by Gwendolyn Burke,
as provided by Shelly Jasperson

She had promised me she'd visit. But I hadn't seen her since she died, and that was weeks ago.

I'd expected a rattling doorknob, a creaking rocking chair. Maybe a translucent, flowing dress with a chilly whisper. But I got bupkis.

Meditation hadn't worked, and Ouija boards were unproductive. It looked like Gran was taking the safe's combination to the afterlife, where it would never help anyone.

In a last-ditch effort, I scheduled a séance.

The medium had asked for Grandma's closest friends and family to attend. But I'd had trouble convincing them to come. The expansive convention center room contained only five people: Sabine, her physical therapist; Gretta, her cycling coach; Yvonne, the girl who took her order every morning at Jo's Java; the medium; and me. It looked like a last-minute bridal shower without the gifts.

The medium, a middle-aged blonde woman whose tan highlighted her wrinkles, surveyed the room and raised a sculpted eyebrow. "Well, I've worked with less."

Gran would have laughed. *Age is an accomplishment!* She would have said. *This woman is hanging on to youth so hard her fake nails might pop off.*

I stifled a giggle. Gran could be so inappropriate.

"It isn't funny. This might not work. Spirits are fickle. Has your grandmother even been to this hotel?"

I nodded. I'd worked the front desk for the past four years, and she'd visited me every Friday with a bag of crumbly cookies and a soda. *Fresh from the oven!* She'd say as she plopped the bag in front of me, so I could clearly read the grocery store label.

Her house would have been ideal, with the huge picture of a cactus and southwest cowboy figurines. Her ancient corduroy recliner had smelled of dusty soap. When I closed my eyes, I could picture her there, leaning on her heirloom safe. In my mind's eye, she tapped the top of it and raised an eyebrow.

But my father owned the house now, and he was remodeling to sell it, the jagweed. Gran would be less welcome there than behind a kissing booth.

I sighed. This would have to do.

Harriet, the medium, flipped off the light switch. Soft light filtered through the translucent curtains in an otherwise dark room.

We sat in cushioned metal chairs around a small, circular table. Candles sat on the plastic surface, flickering underneath an air vent, and a glass of water shivered next to them. I tucked my legs underneath and adjusted my skirt. Gretta and the barista stared at me, expectantly. Sabine grinned at the medium. Were we supposed to hold hands or something?

"Do we all have our questions? Close your eyes. Let's begin." Harriet tucked a blonde hair in place before reaching for my clammy hand. I grasped Sabine's with my other. Her wiry palm, thin and cold, trembled in mine.

Gran's face flashed in my memory. Dusty blue eyes sparkling, thin lips turned upward in a mischievous smile. I grinned. I might really get to see her face soon. And more importantly, get that combination.

Ten million dollars from an old train robbery sat in that safe, passed on from generation to generation. Every time I sat on Gran's wooden futon, I stared at it and pictured the loot inside, shaking my head in wonder. Why hadn't she opened it and used the money? What was she waiting for?

"Grandmother Margaret, we gather tonight with the hope that we'll receive a sign of your presence. Please feel welcome in our circle."

I peeked open my right eye. A candle puffed out.

Harriet continued in an even, soothing voice. "Grandmother Margaret, please let us know you're here by spilling some of the water."

Grandmother Margaret? I didn't know a soul who called her that. Still, chills ran up my spine. The glass tipped over, a deluge splashing onto the table and dousing the candles.

Gretta screamed and stood, but I sighed. I wanted to believe, but the cynic inside me ached to roll my eyes. It seemed fake. This Harriet woman had good reviews, but maybe no one had thought to look under the table for magnets or strings.

"Sit! Do not break the circle!" Harriet's eyes went round and wide.

Gretta cautiously sat back down, her breathing labored.

"If you have questions for Margaret, now is the time to ask. Keep them simple, with only 'yes' or 'no' answers."

Fudge. I didn't know the parameters for ghost questions. I had so much to say and I hadn't been expecting such pomp and circumstance just to talk to my grandmother.

"Uh, Margaret?" Gretta cleared her throat, but her voice remained timorous. "Did you steal my green lipstick?"

I giggled. I could imagine Gran's voice. *The girl had green on her lips, Gwen! What is she, a swamp creature?*

"Margaret, please splash the water for 'yes' and do nothing for 'no'."

We searched each other's eyes. No one worried about closing them anymore. Water splashed onto Gretta's face.

That would have been harder to fake. I sat up straight. Was Gran really here?

"Your turn, Yvonne."

The barista faintly smiled. "Margaret was a great customer. She'd order the same thing and always left me a pile of quarters as a tip."

I raised an eyebrow. "It's not a funeral. Ask her a question."

Yvonne cleared her throat. "Margaret, um, are you happy?"

The water was unexpressive. It appeared she wasn't happy. The woman had had millions within her reach in life, but she'd never been satisfied. She hadn't changed at all.

Sabine licked her lips. "Margaret, I'm sorry to hear you're unhappy. Are you not reunited with your husband?"

I jostled her hand. "You can't ask questions like that. It's misleading."

Besides, Grandfather never made her happy. She was always telling me men were only a means to an end. If the government would just let us clone people, they'd be completely unnecessary. Needless to say, she'd never approved of any of my boyfriends, not even my fiancé.

"Oh." Sabine coughed. "Well, is there food in the afterlife?"

Stagnant water. Not even the faintest ripple. I pursed my lips. That was disappointing. Better eat more tacos while I still could.

Harriet turned to me and nodded.

It was finally my turn. I took a deep breath, not sure how to frame my question. She'd promised to visit. I'd expected an apparition floating through my window or visions in my sleep. This seemed so clinical and impersonal. But it was my only option. I winced and dove right in.

"I broke up with Johnathan." I sighed and pictured Gran in her striped button-down shirt and suspenders, looking like a turn-of-the-century bandit. "Like you told me to. Men only bring disappointment. I get it. So what's the combination?"

Harriet squinted. "Only 'yes' or 'no' questions, please. And could everyone close their eyes?"

A cold breeze drifted across my bare arms, and goosebumps popped on my skin like tiny polka dots.

The water swelled and rushed together to form Gran's head. It flowed around her sharp nose, her under-eye wrinkles. Her hair was more blue and translucent than it had been in life.

I gasped and gripped Sabine and Harriet's hands tighter. They'd better not get scared away now. I was so close.

"Gwen, jeez." Her voice gurgled, like someone speaking underwater. My heart raced. This was it. She'd tell me the combination, and I'd sneak in and open it when Dad was gone. "Why would you do that? You love Johnathan."

"Gran, you told me to! You said I had to if I wanted the combination!"

"Gwennie, I lied about the safe. It's just an old family heirloom. You were supposed to defy your Gran and run off with Johnathan."

I nearly slapped her watery face. The way I'd ended things with Johnathan ... there was no going back. I'd thought I needed to show Gran I was committed.

It couldn't be for nothing. Johnathan and I had been dating for five years. Our hilltop wedding was nearly all planned. Plane tickets were bought. Reservations were made. I couldn't afford to lose all those deposits.

"But the safe ..."

"There's nothing in there but recycled recipes. Gwennie, if I had ten million in a safe, would I crochet my own underwear?"

I cringed, my dreams dripping down to the table with my grandmother's melting head. The remaining water splashed against the plastic tabletop, dousing us like Shamu at SeaWorld.

I'd slapped Johnathan. Told him I couldn't stand him.

"Recipes?" I whispered to no one at all. My grandmother was gone.

Harriet cleared her throat. "That was invigorating!" She dropped my hand and stood up. "I can honestly say I've never had that happen before. You've got an interesting grandmother, Gwen."

"No, wait!" I grabbed her hand. That couldn't be it. Gran didn't tell me anything! "Can we try again?"

Sabine and Gretta sat, blinking. Yvonne's jaw nearly reached her knees. I walked around them to Harriet, who flipped the lights on.

She shook her head. "I'm afraid not. That was a definitive answer if ever I saw one."

"How was I supposed to know Gran was lying? Who would defy a sixty-five-year old woman on her deathbed?"

Harriet shrugged. "Maybe she expected her disapproval would make you defiant. Or that offering you money in exchange for love would disgust you, make you forge your own path, not follow hers."

I fell into the nearest chair. It was pure metal. No cushion. I gripped the sides of the seat with white knuckles, my whole body shivering.

"Speaking of money, I believe we agreed on one-fifty."

Gwendolyn Burke lives in the outskirts of the windiest city in America: Reno, Nevada. For the past four years, she's worked at the Reno Marriott, doling out plastic key cards and silently judging items on room receipts. In her free time, she watches old westerns and may or may not forge bank statements. You can't prove anything.

Shelly Jasperson has an inexplicable love for dead things. This is unrelated to her being a wife, mother of three little terrors, and author. Her short stories can be seen at *Timeless Tales Magazine* and *Bewildering Stories*.

GRAY EYE SHUFFLE

An essay by Othello Maxwell, as provided by Brandon Nolta

———

She looked like the kind of woman for whom doors opened. Tall, hair so black it absorbed the light, her body a pillar of muscle, she strode with confidence through the late-afternoon commuter crowd, someone used to being unimpeded. I watched her walk toward my car, and thought ghosting must have been a tough call for her.

She stopped in front of me, turned her head to meet my gaze. Her eyes were gray, so light they were almost pearl. That's just short of albino in the standard population, and rarer than hen's teeth, as Mom used to say. In Lottos, though, that was almost base model. Eye scans are still the most common way to catch one.

"Double O?" she whispered, body tensed. She seemed poised to run, or maybe kick my head through the train window. I wouldn't blame her for either. Imagine surviving an apocalypse, or being descended from someone who did, only to find that you were now an asset of incalculable value, and everyone wanted a piece—or more—of you. Even the West was shitty about snagging Lottos, and in theory, they still had rights there.

"Yes, ma'am," I whispered back, nodding just a fraction. The whole point of ghosting was to avoid notice. Ghost suits work pretty well at deflecting attention, between the pheromone masks and pupil dilation sensors, but they don't do shit for loud voices or sudden movements. Keep calm and stay unnoticed.

She opened her mouth to say something else, and I held up a finger, pointing at the ceiling. Her eyes flicked upward to the sensor ring in the panel above me. She nodded, and inclined her head toward me, as if we were old friends and not strangers on a trans-Bay of Bengal train.

"Next station," I said, yawning as I did. The older Sikh next to me didn't seem to notice; he probably saw Caucasians with smart lenses talking to themselves all the time, and he'd taken no notice of the ghosting Lotto in front of me. Not that I wanted to test that. I stood as the train began to slow coming into Chennai Port and moved in front of her. No need to watch her leave; she'd follow. Lottos aren't welcome most places, and she'd need help to get somewhere she could be left alone, much less welcomed.

The train stopped, and I headed for the door, eager to get out of the train car I'd been in for the last couple of hours. Vacuum trains are about as fast as you can go without heading into space, but the Bay of Bengal is wide, and getting safely out of Myanmar now is more luck than skill. Bribery still works, but I didn't relax until we'd crossed into Indian Protectorate waters.

The station looked like every other one I've ever been in: cheesy holo-ads, clean but not fanatically so, restrooms and snack bars every 100 meters like clockwork. On the street, the pedestrian population was light, the vehicle traffic slightly less so. Chennai was in good shape compared to northern India, but losing more than a third of its population in two decades left its mark. I looked around at the sidewalk, emptier and cleaner than in my childhood, and felt the ghost's presence at my back. I knew her name—I'd recognized Lieutenant Shrivani Chopra as soon as she looked at me—but decided to let her break that ice.

She didn't say anything until we reached the third and final alley in our roundabout tour of Chennai's finer shitholes. I tapped a quick series of notes, letting the auto-lock read my personalized key, and stood aside, motioning her through the doorway. She stopped right in front of me, looked me right in my ocular implant. "What are you getting out of this?"

"Paid," I said. "What else is there?"

"Easier ways to get paid," she said, shifting her weight slightly. "Safer jobs, in places more welcoming to Americans."

"Am I that obvious?" I asked. I thought my mutt accent was better than that.

She nodded, eyes fixed on mine. If I hadn't known who she was, I'd have thought she was just nervous, instead of ready to beat my ass. Her résumé made for interesting reading, but within arm's reach, the salient point in my HUD was that she was the first front-line female Gurkha, so definitely armed, capable of killing most people, and—if a woman like her was running—in far deeper fathoms of shit than was healthy for me. Which brought me back to her question.

Carefully, I reached up and pulled the smart lenses off my face. Just for show, anyway.

"This one's fake," I said, tapping my left eye with my finger. The iris folded outward, revealing circuitry, which didn't seem to surprise her. "This one's not." I pulled back my eyelid, and quickly hooked the colored contact lens out. Simple but effective, even though any scanner will look past the lens. If they don't think to look, it doesn't matter how good the scan is.

I blinked a couple of times, and met her gaze, the Lotto gray of my real eye matching hers.

Lieutenant Chopra blinked once, twice. Then she smiled.

"Shall we?" I asked.

Together, we went inside to begin sneaking an immortal woman out of India.

~

When the genetic anomalies first started to show up, lots of people thought the stories were bullshit, cooked up by governments too afraid to admit how bad things really were. Losing nearly two billion people will do that. It didn't take long for rumor to become documented fact, though.

Beautiful irony—after years of battle with gene-bombs, crude nanotech, and whatever the skunk works of various nations came up with, the world was left with mountains of corpses and, like a rare orchid growing in a landfill, a new strain of humans. Lottos, they were called, because they'd struck the genetic jackpot: an immune system that could stave off death. Supercharged lymphatics, cells that breezed past the Hayflick limit without metastasizing, every filter and recycling system in the body cranked up to just short of magic. Lottos could eat trash, drink toxic waste, and adapt to all of it. A Lotto could drink a mug of Ebola and maybe develop a temporary rash; a needle full of HIV did nothing at all.

Of course, they were still vulnerable to the usual. Fire, bullets, plane crashes, and knives would kill a Lotto just as dead as a regular human. Or so everyone thought, until a Lotto in Johannesburg walked out of a hospital morgue four hours after dying in a hotel fire, naked and surprised but apparently unharmed. Short of completely dismembering the brain, a Lotto could heal from damn near anything. That was when Lottos became hunted, and I found a new career.

Grow up military, and you get used to making your way around quick. If you have a talent for languages, a face made for ghosting, and the ability to speak softly until you need the big stick, smuggling might be for you. There's money in moving everything from cigarettes to prosthetics, but the big change is in moving Lottos to one of the three safe places left: Australia, New Liberia, and Taiwan. My client, who was once a cultural attaché based in Sydney, knew where she wanted to go, and for the money she paid, I was going to get her there.

We walked inside the tin-walled hideaway and entered a long hallway, covered in some spots, connecting to a dozen other shacks, huts, and occasional real buildings. I led her through the maze, navigating by smell and memory, until we found Aziq's shop. It looked like any other door, although a little more purple than the rest, but my artificial eye picked up the flycams and tripwires easily enough. Probably meant there were traps I couldn't see; I made sure to approach slowly, with cash and ID easily visible in the mottled sunlight from the gaps in the roof.

I heard a clicking sound, and from the way she shifted, so did my client. "Double O, who's your friend?" a voice asked.

"Fellow traveler," I said. "Needs some vacation time."

"We aim to please," the voice said, and Aziq's purple door swung open. Together, my client and I strode in, letting our eyes adjust to the lack of illumination in Aziq's shop. Shelves of random parts, LEDs, and devices too damaged to identify were propped against the walls, reaching to the ceiling, maybe holding it up. Every flat surface was covered with technical manuals, news prints, food wrappers, and well-used tools, and one wall was almost completely covered with scavenged plasma and LCD monitor screens. The floor was wall-to-wall static matting, spotlessly clean and almost glistening.

"Just for show," my client said, looking at the floor. I nodded. She had a good eye. Aziq's real business was a little deeper into the rat's nest.

"Aziq's in the blending business," I said.

My client reached to her left and knocked a stack of old wrappers and what looked like Soviet-era invoices onto the floor, sending up a pillar of dust smelling of seared lamb and mango. The mess scattered over the floor, carpeting the entryway in old paperwork.

"Glad to help," she said.

I smiled and led her back to Aziq's real shop. Behind a ratty tapestry that Gandhi might have had a picnic on in his youth, a hermetically sealed door was jammed into the wall. The door's sensor plate scanned us, and we were rewarded with a whoosh of pressure as the door opened. Holding the door open for my client, I followed her into the shop/lab.

"Lieutenant Chopra, it's an honor to meet you," Aziq said, bowing slightly as he spoke. His bald head seemed to glow in the fluorescent light. Around us, a ring of 3-D printers and blade racks loomed from ceiling to false floor, under which snaked miles of cables and connections. Rumor was that Aziq had the fifth-largest data center in eastern India.

"You know who I am," my client asked. Her expression was pleasant, but her eyes were hard.

I remembered that I didn't know where her kukri was, or if she had more than one.

"I worked with a company of Gurkhas in Sri Lanka, some time ago. Your op in Pakistan was popular water cooler gossip for a time. You have more friends than you know, Lieutenant."

She smiled. "Maybe I'll meet them someday."

Aziq smiled in return, the corners of his mouth barely twitching under his meticulously groomed mustache. "All good things in due time. Come, please have a seat. The databank search may take a few more minutes. You may as well be comfortable."

A moment's search produced two office chairs, and we sat while Aziq pulled a stool up to a home-built workstation, a stack of consumer-grade PCs wired in parallel. For the better part of two hours, we watched Aziq in his element, hiding searches and back-door data dumps behind a forest of shell accounts, zombie accesses, and the occasional social engineering hack. Slowly, my client's new identity, clean and free of any reason for government attention, took shape in Aziq's hands. I'd seen Aziq work before, and I was still impressed.

As evening started to fall, the last forged smart doc emerged from the printer, and we were done. Physically, we weren't buying much: a few smart docs, a passport with ID chip, and a couple of bankcards hooked to artificially aged accounts. Aziq bowed as I paid him and walked us out through a different door. When we stepped outside again, we were three blocks north of the alleyway.

"How far can we trust these?" she asked me as we walked toward a bus kiosk. Street buses still took cash, and I figured we had to wait an hour or so to let the new ID wend its way through Protectorate systems.

"Aziq hasn't screwed a client yet, but let's not push it. Your face is still relatively well-known, and a ghost suit won't do diddly against high-focus surveillance."

"No shopping sprees, then."

"No," I laughed.

She looked down the road at the wheezing metal box making its way toward us. Looked like it still used diesel, and might have been brought by the British. Still, it was mostly empty, and wouldn't have much surveillance. "How do you plan to get us out of the country?"

"Hope you don't get seasick."

Lieutenant Chopra didn't look thrilled. I made a note to give her Dramamine before she boarded the cargo ship. She didn't know how fortunate she was, getting to ride in a tub with actual passenger compartments, but telling her that probably wouldn't help.

With a clank and a whoosh of exhaust, the rickety bus stopped, and the driver, who was old when the bus was new, cranked open the door. We climbed aboard, and found seats toward the back of the bus, a couple rows behind a quiet family and a sullen city policeman uninterested in everything but sleeping.

I went over the plan again as the bus lurched back onto the road. Arrangements to ship the lieutenant out on a New Liberia-registered cargo ship were set, but the captain would need an additional bribe to not turn my client in. Once the ship entered international waters, I'd trip an Aziq special: an alert that the lieutenant was seen in a little cafe near Jammu, close to Pakistan.

Maybe the Protectorate goons would buy it, but either way, it would muddy the waters. Once the ship reached Jakarta, a fisherman friend related to half of Java would pick her up and island-hop her all the way to Papua New Guinea, then put her on a private flight into Sydney. I'd had clients successfully make this trip before, so I was only mostly worried.

"Two questions," she said as the bus turned onto the wide road to the docks.

I nodded; most clients were not as cooperative, so I felt like I owed her a little something.

"What does Double O stand for?" she said.

"Othello," I said. "My dad heard the name once, thought it was great for a girl."

"Did no one point out the character is a man?"

"He didn't care about that. Finding out the original was black, something else."

She laughed, a low throaty sound that didn't carry far. The policeman stirred in his seat, then slumped against the window again. I looked at the road ahead. In the distance, I could see the stop approaching, and beyond that, the entrance to the cargo docks, where some of our fellow riders were likely going to work.

"Very well, Othello, although your given name is far better than your nickname."

"There's another meaning to it. It comes from an old movie series, something about spies. My parents thought it was funny."

She nodded, pursed her lips. I thought I knew what her second question might be. Proving my Lotto nature was usually good enough, but I suspected my proof would raise another issue.

Before she could frame the question, the bus chuffed and rattled to a stop at the first dockside station. We got to our feet and shuffled down the aisle. Nobody looked twice. The policeman slept through the entire stop.

I started to walk toward the docks, mentally counting off the ships until we reached the New Liberian freighter, and a firm hand closed around my upper arm. My client looked sternly at me. My krav maga is good, but not good enough. I waited.

The lieutenant took a deep breath. "Why are you lying about being a Lotto?"

I thought about how to answer. Damn, she was observant. Wrong conclusion, but she didn't have all the info. I put my hand over hers. "I didn't lie, Lieutenant. You just don't have the whole picture."

"Explain, please," she said, in a tone that didn't sound like a request.

Gently, I took her arm. "I'll do better. Come on."

I led her around the side of the squat office building that fronted the main entrance. We walked to the first door, which opened to reveal a dilapidated restroom. An "out of order" sign was nailed to the door, but that was fine. I'd scouted this place; it had lights and a mirror, which was all I needed. I ushered her inside and locked the door behind us.

"I'm going to reach inside my pack now," I said. "I assume you have a kukri on you?"

"Two," she said.

"OK, well, you don't need them. Just watch," I said.

I took out my med kit, unrolled it on the counter next to the sink. By habit, I inventoried what I had: three full vials of my latest compound, a hypogun, a full set of surgical scalpels, and two packs of disinfectant. More than enough, as long as I got the mix right. Too little methotrexate, too much generic glucocorticoid, things could get uncomfortable.

"Let's not assume anything here. Why do you think I'm not a Lotto?" I asked as I loaded a vial into the hypogun.

"Your artificial eye," she said, gaze locked onto my arms and shoulders. Waiting for me to grab for something, I figured.

"Because it would regrow, right?" I said. "Even if I'd lost the eye before those genes went active." I swabbed a patch on my upper arm, and pressed the hypogun nozzle against my skin. The trigger fired automatically at the correct pressure, made to be as idiot-proof as possible.

Lieutenant Chopra nodded.

"Therefore," I said, "if I have an artificial eye, I'm not a Lotto, no matter what other signs may present. My eye color could be due to albinism or injury, and some conditions can mimic common Lotto genetic expressions. Logical?"

"I agree," the lieutenant said.

"Best disguise there is for a Lotto," I said, washing my hands in disinfectant. The scalpels got a heavy spray, and a quick scan confirmed the blades were as clean as could be in a Chennai restroom without plumbing. My real eye couldn't do that.

"Lotto traits often run in families," I said. "Any of your family come up lucky besides you?"

"No, though I had an uncle who disappeared suddenly when I was in training," she said thoughtfully. "I am the first confirmed."

"My parents didn't have it," I said, holding a scalpel up to the light. "My brother did, though." I handed her the scalpel handle first to hold while I went through the removal procedure for my artificial eye. "So did my daughter."

She breathed in sharply, but said nothing. Nothing to say, really. Many normal people had similar tales; Lottos just had them with a side order of dread. It just made it harder to look at other Lottos and not see her face, her eyes, or hear her infant cries as they pulled her from my arms.

"Hold this so that it faces me," I told her. "This mirror is filthy."

Lieutenant Chopra did as I said. The wireless connection was good; I could see myself clearly, including the ocular tissue regrowing along the interior wall of the socket. From the tingling in my fingers, the immunosuppressants were taking effect. I still had another minute or so before I could switch out the vials and shoot analgesic spray into the socket. One of the downsides of being a Lotto is that painkillers don't work well. For what was next, though, painkillers were essential. My knowledge was hard-earned.

The tingling turned into a low hum, not unpleasant but strange. I loaded the analgesic into the hypogun, turned the setting to spray, and coated the interior of my eye socket. Then I did it again. Cold needling turned to numbness, and within a few seconds, it was as if the socket was no longer there.

"Between the immunosuppressants and my artificial eye's housekeeping, I can keep the eye from coming back quickly," I told her as I pulled a pair of microforceps from the med kit. "I am a Lotto, though. It will grow back, and the cocktails only work for so long. Mixing a new compound takes time."

"And so—" the lieutenant began.

"And so," I said, "occasionally, I have to cut."

Gently, I reclaimed the scalpel from my unwitting assistant. I pressed the blade against the socket rim, checking for sensitivity to pressure or cold. Good to go.

"We'd better hurry," I said. "Your ship leaves soon."

I recognized the look in the lieutenant's eyes. Every time I think of my child, I remember it in mine. Thus thinking of my daughter, I began cutting out my eye again.

Born into a military family, Othello Maxwell (or Double O, as she prefers) is a world traveler, jack of all trades, and professional Lotto smuggler. Not much of her early life is known, and what details she does share are carefully parsed to minimize exposure. What is known, however, is that she's good at her work, has contacts all over the surviving First World countries, and counts ancient movie trivia and recreational immunology amongst her few hobbies.

Brandon Nolta is a writer, editor, and professional curmudgeon living in the transportation-challenged wilds of north Idaho. After earning an MFA, he went slightly mad. Nothing much happened with that, so he gave it up and started working for respectable companies again, which he still does when he wants to pay his bills. His fiction and poetry have appeared in *The Centropic Oracle*, *Stupefying Stories*, *The Pedestal Magazine*, *Every Day Fiction*, *Perihelion*, and a cacophony of other publications. *Iron and Smoke*, his first novel, was published by Montag Press in 2015; he has yet to admit to a second.

WITHIN THE PULSE OF DARKNESS

An essay by Cassius Carrington, as provided by Lucas Leery

———————————

Dear Cass,

I invite you to assist me on my next expedition. The site is in remote, northern land that I trust you will remember well. Your task will be simple: to record data thoroughly and accurately.

I apologize, but I cannot share more. You must understand the significance of this project. Please keep my offer private, as my research is of a most sensitive nature.

I leave Thursday.

Kent

~

Though we had been friends since childhood, Kent's proposition was strictly business. The letter nonetheless excited me, snapped my thoughts from the doldrums of my daily routine. Despite its vagueness, I accepted his offer in hopes of reconnecting with a friend lost to time. The letter was stark and abrupt, much like the writer himself, but I sensed in its language something as close to a plea as ever a man like Kent could make. Somehow, though I had not heard from him in over a decade, I felt a responsibility to respond. Besides, the trip was an excuse for escape, if but brief, from my life as a bachelor in the city, a situation I found exceedingly tedious as the years wore on me.

Kent worked as a geobiologist studying the evolution of Earth's relationship with life. Though we had fallen largely out of touch since our schooldays, I kept up to date on his studies by following

65

him in academic publications. In recent years, however, his name had disappeared from headlines, and I assumed that he had taken his career elsewhere. I myself, a former laboratory technician who now struggled as a freelance science journalist, was surprised to hear that he still practiced research in the field.

I was not surprised, however, that he had chosen me for his companion. We grew up together exploring deep within those northern reaches, woods I once knew more intimately than anyone alive. Moreover, I pursued science seriously enough to make a career of it, was familiar with equipment and repairs, and was a trustworthy, if not predictable, friend. Besides, I was a budding science journalist. He made it clear from the start that he intended the story of this expedition to make headlines.

~

We were not an hour on the road when the weather turned. Kent drove through the downpours with no apparent thought for delaying our journey and despite my attempts at conversation would not be distracted from the road. Due to his solemn demeanor, inklings of regret already began to creep across my thoughts.

He had always been a stoic man. His features were sharp and angular with a jaw perpetually defined by a shadow of stubble. His long nose had a slight bend where it had been broken as a boy. He was the tallest of our class yet always had loose clothes that gave his height a kind of ghostly, looming quality. Even growing up he had a gravity about him, a contemplative sobriety I had admired, but seeing him now after all these years, paled by the gray light of the road, I recognized a change. The lines of his face were more severe, deeper than a man his age should have, and his eyes, which had always been dark and piercing, were blacker and more intense. His knuckles, I noticed, whitened on the wheel as the sky steadily darkened.

It was deep dusk by the time we reached the point at which the road became impassable by car. Despite the rain and my partner's disposition, I strove to keep my spirits high and forgive his preoccupations. Though he was stern in regard to the professional nature of our trip, I anticipated sharing drink, laughs, and memories once settling into camp.

In my years as a technician, I had never before seen anything like the instruments Kent had packed. Along with basic water and soil sampling gear was an array of sophisticated honing devices, colorimeters, and complex sensing systems with long antennae that protruded from our packs. Methodically he wrapped them for protection within enormous coils of rope, the purpose of which was at that point a mystery to me. One contraption in particular caught my eye for its elaborate system of beeping lights, though I knew better than to ask. After all, my place was as documentarian, not scientist, and I refrained from embarrassing myself with questions that would only expose me as an amateur and disrupt Kent's concentration.

We waded through the growing darkness, our packs covered and our hoods pulled low. With increasing frequency, Kent paused to scrutinize the data on his instruments until suddenly we veered off the road into the brush. By this time, we had strapped headlamps about our hoods and only the branches within the bouncing circles of our beams were visible. It irked me then how the darkness tangled beyond our light seemed more and more to tighten its grip, how our vision seemed ever shrinking in the density of such night.

What minimal conversation there was had ceased upon leaving the vehicle. Other than the occasional directional beeping of Kent's instruments, the woods were eerily still. In fact, the night was so static and black that I succumbed to a habit I developed as a boy, alone and scared in the woods at night. Then, I would convince myself of voices throbbing within unseen grottoes, indistinctly swathing me in a choir of my name. These voices, natural manipulations of night sounds and projections of internal fears, were of the kind that terrorize young boys and leave them afraid to breathe, paralyzed within their sleepless bedrolls. Now a rational man many years beyond that childish fear of the dark, I had altogether outgrown such anxieties and ignored the sounds. The longer the night wore on, however, the farther my mind wandered into whispered choirs and muted drums that summoned me through the tortuous brush.

I am not one for complaining, particularly on excursions in the elements. I was brought up to worship the wild and hold myself to be a high-quality outdoorsman, but to press on through raw, midnight rain tested me. More than once I stopped to demand that we make camp for the night or that Kent explain his mission, but something in the look about him propelled me forward without a word. The torchlight split his face in a way that obscured his eyes, revealing only the fixed line of his mouth and clenched jaw, and his looming figure, clad with poncho and pack, was shapeless and grotesque in the blackness. Still, it was not that Kent intimidated me, but that I sensed in him a pleading dedication, if not possessed determination, that provoked me to continue. It is as though by recognizing his enthusiasm, his craving for results, I became an equally motivated accomplice in the mission, fascinated by the intention of which I was miserably ignorant.

We had not been in the woods long when I found that my wristwatch had frozen. Blaming faulty batteries and moisture, I pocketed it and tried to ignore a gnawing feeling of nakedness. But my inability now to track the time nagged me and gave me an unsettling sense of detachment from the outside world, a notion of helplessness I had to consciously fight from consuming my thoughts. Swiftly now the night darkened, and the brush thickened around me.

I am unsure exactly how many hours passed, but the plod seemed to drag on for more time than could fit within one night. Eventually, after deliberating with his nameless machine, Kent motioned for me to push through a thicket just west of where we stooped dripping in our momentary pause. Upon splitting open a path wide enough for one man and a pack, I entered a place unlike any I had before experienced. A cleared circle opened, and I could tell by the abrupt ceasing of my lamplight that a cliff gaped before us. The rain broke suddenly, and the moon exposed itself for the first time, a pale orb dimmed beneath torn shrouds of mist. In the peeling light, I dropped my pack and approached the cliff. The enormity of what I beheld stunned me. I think if Kent had not grabbed my shoulders that I would have plunged over the edge right then and there.

Staggering on the ledge, I moved my torch to follow the rim of the cliff extending in both directions. Steadily the edges curved inward. I watched the dot of my headlamp bounce weakly on a surface of rock directly across from where I stood and realized with shock that I teetered not on the face of a cliff, but on the edge of a terrible hole. As I followed the wall downward, my light disappeared within its descent, swallowed by a lurking blackness.

From my estimations, the chasm was roughly circular, about sixty meters in diameter and immeasurably deep. It was as though, and I propose this without lightness or jest, the hole was not drilled from the surface by man, but carved outward by some awful industrious species born from the earth itself.

It was here, amidst anxiety and darkness upon the edge of the chasm, that notions of regret for accepting Kent's offer began to take hold. That so easily he could have let me fall off the cliff angered me, and I began suddenly to resent my partner for his solemnness and silence, by which I now felt endangered. Then, with more vigor, I turned my resentment toward myself. I recognized the direness of my situation, how, without knowing our location, assignment, or even the time, I was completely dependent on a man who had essentially become a stranger to me. What is worse, I had no one but myself to blame for so easily letting Kent use me for his benefit. The more I thought, the more deeply I understood the severity of my condition. I knew no solution to my predicament, no possible comfort for my worries, and with no one to talk to, I felt trapped within my own dark mind.

This is why when Kent wordlessly adjusted his equipment and set out to survey the site, I elected to stay back and set up camp. The idea of venturing along the ledge petrified me, and the fact that Kent had chosen to do so with the same reticent commitment that prodded us through the woods only compounded my resentment for him. Yet as his torch diminished in the distance, I discovered solitude to be a terror more unbearable than strained companionship. As quickly as the moon cast its pallor upon the clearing did clouds return to suffocate all trace of lightness. The vague beginnings of song again hummed lightly in my mind, and my dread eventually spurred me to rush to Kent's side. Without the moon, our headlamps were futile against such impenetrable blackness, but Kent would not be swayed to delay his investigation. I felt even more powerless in the face of his determination.

Kent's company offered little to relieve my anxiety. He still did not say a word, and though I felt the aching need to break the silence, I could not bring myself to speak first. I walked beside him, exercising tedious prudence for what would have proven a fatal misstep, and in vain I urged myself to gain the courage to speak. My resentment toward him grew with every silent step until soon I stopped wanting him to speak altogether, believing that the longer he went without words, the more certain I could be of his cruel intentions.

Continuously I checked my naked wrist and continuously endured the unease of being out of touch with time. I constantly expected our packs to appear and our survey to conclude, but still we pressed on. Though I knew our route was a circle, the farther we walked, the farther I felt we ventured into depths from which we could not return. I began to worry that our packs would be indecipherable in the thickness of the night, that we would walk forever through the darkness in a never-ending circle around the hole. Still I walked on, terrified to continue but thoroughly unwilling to break from my course.

The fear that so steadily grew within me seemed to imitate the darkness emanating from the chasm. I felt it where it tugged at the edges of my consciousness. Eventually self-scrutiny seized my mind, and Kent no longer mattered. My thoughts shifted from the present, and I contemplated what I now recognized to be the stagnant cycle of my daily existence: waking, working, sleeping, waking, all the while moving closer and closer to death. Every step along the brim of the abyss drilled the awareness of my pathetic existence deeper into my consciousness.

And the deeper these thoughts plunged, the more my fear transgressed into a black and spiraling frenzy, a maelstrom mimicking my worry that we had actually been circling the hole for hours, making countless trips about the perimeter while inching closer toward its tremendous rim. I felt my course bound as though upon a magnetized track, and I saw myself now distant from Kent, who eventually ceased to exist entirely. This sensation of solitude and doom, that I had walked myself into a slow-moving vortex steadily ripping me to the depths of my fate, became so real in my mind that I felt a crippling panic well from within me. I saw my life rutted in a steepening course, dropping to darkness resonant with soft and terrible choirs, and I heard a pounding like some muffled drum grown quicker and louder, quicker and louder within the pulse of my sickened thoughts.

Eventually it became too much. In a wave of sudden clarity, I determined that nothing could qualify my life as livable. I resented myself for finding any part of my tedious existence worthwhile and hated the fact that I had wasted myself on living for so long. All at once, I saw humankind to be a child lying in wait for his mother to sing him to sleep. To my horror, that feeling of doom so overwhelmed me that I abruptly resolved to embrace the song and plunge my soul into infinite darkness, to realize immediately the fate of man rather than endure the torture of inching ever near it.

Yet just before I broke the trance and hurled myself over the brink, Kent's voice salvaged my thoughts: "Here we are. Better make camp."

Through the pounding of my shaken heartbeat, I muttered in response and splayed my pack on a tarp. While Kent set to adjusting his equipment, I tried to distract myself by preparing a fire, though I failed to make the matches take. All the papers I scrapped together glowed only momentarily in streaks of heat, succumbing quickly to darkness as though swallowed by the night. Either my shuddering nerves or some violent element of the place refused a flame. I was quick to give up hope.

Finding some comfort in the thought of rest, I proceeded to build my tent with an absent mind and trembling hands. I then assisted Kent in sheltering the equipment, which he had organized around his prized contraption. Just as we had secured the tarp, the drizzle turned to a bitter sleet that bounced from our hoods and collected in the creases of our coats. Without so much as "good night" we crawled into our tents.

I lay awake with my torch swinging from the roof and heard Kent outside tampering once more with the machine. It was with the soft patter of ice and the distant sound of unknown instruments that I drifted into uneasy sleep, my light casting strange pallor through the canvas walls. The darkness was an enemy I resolved not to let enter the safety of my tent.

Teetering there on the brink of sleep, my mind sunk to fears of that depthless hole, and I drifted into dream-induced awe of its profundity, dreading what again seemed my inevitable draw into the overwhelming power of its blackness. And as I lay there, perhaps asleep already, the same distant choir edged upon my consciousness, a lullaby that softened my dread and replaced it with feelings not altogether unlike comfort.

~

To my delight, I slept through the night, awaking to the abrupt scrape of ice sheets sliding off my tent. Ashamed of my previous night's behavior, I determined to approach the day and my partner's assignment with a new perspective, blaming my emotional weakness on stress and a lack of sleep. The outside world was ashen with a mist that rolled about the clearing and made it impossible to tell the time of day. Though the appearance of the place was certainly tamer, the pervasive aura of unnaturalness had not altogether dwindled with the rising of the sun. The sleet that had accumulated in, the night now covered the ground, trees and tents with a ghostly frost, and in conjunction with the mist, it refracted daylight in a dull pallor that fused earth and sky in disorienting lightness. There lurked as though within the fog itself a quality of sickliness, and I consistently worked to quell that pervasive notion of unease.

Following the tones of Kent's instruments to the edge of the hole, I found him busy at the rim. Though I wished to keep my distance, I willed myself to approach the ledge and offer my assistance. The winds from within the hole made me shiver, and I noted, swallowing my fear, how the blackness emanating from the depths seemed palpably to devour the colorless light of day. It was as though that darkness was a living beast, perhaps an infinite pack of beasts, and it swarmed from the abyss to nip fiercely at surrounding light, consuming the very air within the void that was its only substance. Standing several yards away, I felt that awful pull on my thoughts, and I saw myself edge upon an inner, more terrible darkness than what my eyes beheld. A pit opened within my stomach.

"Hand me a flare."

Kent's voice wakened me to the world beyond the chasm, and I became aware of the tools and equipment littering the granite ledge. His nameless contraption had grown in the night and was now equipped with shoulder straps and a leather harness. Two massive spotlights straddled its topmost antennae like the eyes of a wraithlike beast.

I found the flares within a pile of equipment and approached Kent with calculated steps, kneeling beside him as he loaded and fired a round into the hole. The flames died with startling abruptness, as when a candle is stifled by wetted fingers in a hushed and darkened room. He lobbed another over the center of the hole. It was extinguished before it crested to descent, leaving in its sudden absence a well of darkness impenetrable even in the light of day.

That dying flare mimicked for me some element intrinsic to my humanity, and it was all I could do to prevent myself from sliding into that loathsome vortex that tortured me the night before. I crawled away from the ledge and shut my eyes, fighting the black thoughts that whorled within me. When I opened them, I realized with renewed horror why he brought me here.

The three antennae that so baffled me on our journey into camp protruded from the instrument's topmost section and toned periodically with yellow and red flashes. The spotlights were fastened below them, their lenses reinforced with caging and the bulbs, faintly visible through layers of glass, the largest I had ever seen. On closer inspection, I perceived that each bulb housed a team of hundreds of smaller bulbs organized as a complex union of filament and glass. A strap descended from the padded panel below these lights and from it hung a helmet rigged with goggles, a respirator, a microphone and an additional headlight. From the lower shoulder protruded a retractable arm upon which a screen was fastened. The screen, equipped with a number of labeled buttons and controls, corresponded to various devices for measuring depth, temperature, pressure, color, humidity, wind speed, and radiation.

From the shoulder straps hung various tools: a pick adze, long-handled tongs, a walkie-talkie, two handheld flashlights, a compass, and a whistle. From the waist belt hung two massive coils of rope, another flare gun with packets of flares, three additional flashlights, a knife, sheathed, and a small first aid kit. The attached harness was of the kind that climbers wear and was well equipped with titanium karabiners, small rope loops, and detachable connection straps that bound it to the overall unit. On its side were two more compartments, one a housing for additional batteries and a repair kit and the other a data storage locker I recognized to be pressurized with an airtight seal.

"Kent," I managed to stutter from the depths of my sickness. "You've lost your mind."

He was jotting messages in a pocket notebook and for a long time did not make any sign of recognition. I wondered then whether he could perceive life beyond the abyss or if he had fallen so deep within the vortex of astonishment that his fellow man had become a mere instrument in his exploration.

Finally he turned and approached me. His eyes were not on me but on the terrible apparatus whose tones strengthened as the morning wore past.

"Do not try to persuade me," he said, caressing the edges of his machine. "There's no use. I brought you to do a job, not to be a friend."

I stepped carefully backward to increase the distance between us, between me and that awful abyss.

"This site is everything. Since I first found it I knew what my research would entail. I've spent years studying it but have failed to retrieve data that means anything. Half a dozen universities have rejected me and twice that number of research teams have cursed me. They vow never to return. My former partner disappeared here. His body was never recovered, and my funding was never renewed. I understand the fear, all of it, but how can I explain it to a board of professionals? Without data, science cannot conceptualize what happens here."

He stopped adjusting his equipment and looked at me for what seemed like the first time. His voice lowered and something vague about him changed, as though he was pleading with me to believe in him, begging, as a friend, that I would relate to his fascination and understand the sad delirium I know now that plagued him. He leaned slightly toward me as though to confide some personal insecurity, and his posture shifted to that of a child flailing for reassurance. His stature seemed shrunken. He spoke in a slow, deliberate whisper.

"Something is in that hole," he said. "It's not an animal, but it's so much more than rock, water, and air. I have felt its pulse. There's life within it, a form of the likes that science has no language to understand. It lurks somewhere between the darkness and the air. We can't know more than what's proven, but I feel that this thing, this *being*, is vast and sentient and moves with the fluidity of darkness itself. It is silent and invisible, survives on the absence of light, and acts with a force that flexes on the human psyche. Its black wind, my partner would claim, preys on the mind, strangles the will for life and wrenches the spirit into a vortex of delusion. I have seen it, I have felt it, and I have fought it every moment since the day I found it.

"I am not a superstitious man. I don't believe in the lore of mysticism but in the systematic methods of science. But without evidence, my critics are right to laugh. As of now, my subject fails to exist in the material world. It's just a spirit of improvable myth. My name is tarnished. Former colleagues call me mad. They blame me for my partner's death. They claim I'm in the science of dark arts, that my studies are more concerned with the supernatural, the fantastical, and the spiritual than the physical. Which is why I chose you: you have nothing to lose, but everything to gain. When my research publishes, it will change the natural field of inquiry, forever."

"Kent—"

"I assure you, I am not mad. This is not a plea. Today you are to help me quantify this darkness and debunk the myths. That is what men of science do. I will die if only to prove my research has not been in vain, to pioneer a breakthrough and quantify what pulses beneath the earth.

"You have a choice, not as a friend, but as a scientist. Either stay to record the making of history, or leave me alone, risking the loss of my findings. I can't make you stay, but know that nothing you do will stop me from entering the dark."

I will never fully rationalize my decision. Reeling from disbelief and recovering still from wretches of panic, I learned that desperation possesses a potential for persuasion that exceeds violent coercion. Perhaps because of our childhood friendship or my aversion for dispute, or perhaps because some curious part of me also craved an answer despite or, God forbid, *due to* the consequences, I wanted to support my friend, and I wanted to trust what he told me. I would like to believe that Kent reached the scientist within me, the part that craved answers and needed to see experiments through, but not a day has passed that I have since feared it was instead some darker element of my nature that drove me to stand by and witness what I knew to be the imminent destruction of human spirit.

Regardless, I stayed. Forever the observer, I stood stone still while Kent resumed rifling through his gear, finalizing details for his exploration. He then unfolded from his pack a reflective suit and stepped delicately into it, zipping the chest closed to make a seal around his neck. I was entranced, staring into the abyss from a safer distance and feeling its darkness tug at my spirit. Before any time had passed, he spoke.

"You hold the radio. I will relay measurements for you to transcribe every thirty meters of depth. The audio box will record our communications, but you must document everything in writing. I am not willing to take any risk in losing this data."

He shoved the two-way receiver into my hand and walked off with one end of the enormous rope, wrapping it about the trunk of a spruce and belaying it to a nearby boulder jutting from the undergrowth.

"I have rigged a pulley system to my belay line and will hoist up samples of air, rock or water, whatever is down there, for testing at the lab. All that I ask is for you to remove the canisters and pile them a safe distance from the edge. In the event of communication failure, I will haul myself to the brim, sending a message on the pulley rig for you to help me resurface."

With that he donned his contraption, the beeps of which had sped to a constant drone, buckled his helmet, and spoke a message into his radio. The automatic recording device at my feet simultaneously blinked and stamped the log with the baseline "0 HRS 0 MIN 0 SEC 0 M." Before I could speak, he heaved the rope over the brim, rocked his heels on the edge, and rappelled himself backward. He did not so much as look at me as he dropped himself over what might well have been the brink of infinite night.

Immediately he was out of sight, the hum of his instruments silenced. For the first time, I felt the stillness of the clearing. Breezes whispered through high spruce boughs, and in the airy distance, a trunk creaked lightly. Far off, a wood thrush fluted. From where I stood at a safe distance from the edge, I was startled to see the dim flash of his spotlights when he switched them on, though they too receded abruptly into nothingness. In my mind, I heard the gently throbbing echo of song.

It seemed a long time before Kent's voice crackled through the radio to report on his surroundings: "Everything in check at negative thirty meters; walls sheer and granite; winds increasing from below; temperature rising to five degrees; radiation levels normal; will relay report from next checkpoint. Is the equipment set up top? Over."

The recorder flashed and incorrectly stamped the log with its label: "0 HRS 0 MIN 0 SEC 30 M." I found the error peculiar but not noteworthy and responded in the affirmative, to which Kent ended the conversation. The radio silenced once more.

He checked in with similar notes for the next several hundred meters. Though the composite of the walls changed only subtly, other details progressed consistently. Humidity and temperatures rose drastically, while wind gusts accelerated to levels that forced Kent to shout his measurements into the receiver. Every one hundred fifty meters he extracted samples of rock and stored them in his pack.

"Report from negative 450 meters: pegmatite walls enriched with beryl; winds 136 kilometers per hour; temperature 58 degrees; radiation normal; sending 10-centimeter sample of pegmatite for analysis. Over."

Due to the steadily worsening conditions, the lapse between Kent's calls grew progressively longer, though the recording device defectively refuted the passing of time. My nerves grew between radio checkpoints and, though I strove to resist, I felt my thoughts spiraling to those same sensations of doom that panicked me on the previous night. The deeper Kent descended and the longer I waited at the edge of the chasm, the more difficult it became for me to remain lucid. I closed my eyes and saw myself churning through the tortuous descent of my life, flailing uselessly as the hollow world spun me downward to my doom. Repeatedly I found myself reeling on the rock, crawling closer to the rim of the abyss, whispering nervous nonsense, and receding incrementally deeper into the void of my own black thoughts. By the time Kent was eight hundred meters down, I was slowly scrabbling along the edge of the chasm, inching toward the pit and feeling through the fits of my mind the weight of darkness' heavy pull. Each time, it was Kent's voice that shattered my delirium and wrenched me rushing back to the safety of the woodside.

"Still with you down 960 meters. Walls sheer and very smooth quartz; winds 152; temperature 64. No sign of a base. I will continue descent. Over."

When he spoke, I could only picture him thrashing like a paper doll, dropping like a single grain of sand into the blackened hourglass of eternity. The conditions he endured were astonishing, but he never once uttered a word of complaint. It was as though the project so consumed him that he no longer had regard for his physical body. All that mattered to him was collecting data. The darkness thickened, and my mental state worsened.

At negative fifteen hundred meters, the pack's sample locker reached capacity, forcing Kent to extract one final sample before sending the lot to the surface. The rock at that depth had become a variety of the likes he had never before encountered, yet his tools were ineffectual at piercing its façade. After a great effort, he finally settled on providing a detailed description, marking the vital importance of returning with more aggressive instruments to conduct extraction. His account of the stone represents the first significant evidence of his mind loosening its grip on the expedition's professional nature.

"This is something. It is beautiful. Science must see this. Nothing I have heard of matches the substance of this rock. It feels as though it has been wave-washed over such a vast expanse of time that all exterior particles have worn away and only the very heart of rock, the innermost element of its existence, remains. To touch it sends waves of impact through my veins. It is of a horrifying hue. Its color matches that of my surroundings within the cavern, a blackness that would blanch anything previously conceived of by science. The walls and the darkness between them are latent with something like electricity. I feel it pulsing within me. Its weight is momentous, its beauty hypnotizing, its blackness purer than any substance of the known natural world. Everything has changed. I must descend."

At that, his voice was overtaken by the wind, and soon thereafter, his radio cut out altogether. Despite my frenzied efforts to contact him, to plead with him to resurface or at least to send the samples, Kent did not respond. It was as though his radio had been switched off, and I was now subject to a new level of silence within the dwindling daylight about me. Very quietly I perched at the woodside, clutching my knees and holding my breath as nighttime seemed slowly to seep over the brim of the abyss, ever so slightly deepening the greyness of the air. I feared the extent of my soul's loneliness. From far off within the darkness, I perceived the beating of muted drums, and voices began faintly to beckon me in song. The recording device blinked and stamped zeros on its time log.

He radioed at negative twenty-one hundred meters but was deaf to my attempts to inform him of the radio malfunction. Though he continued to relay data, it had lost all structure and had deteriorated into a string of meaningless figures and wild observations. He spoke of a violent wind, of rubber melting off his goggles and of walls too dense to hope for further samples. He continued on and conditions only worsened. His calls became more sporadic.

Down what the instruments recorded as nearly twenty-five hundred meters, he radioed to describe markings he discovered on the rock face. He neglected to give any information regarding conditions, but instead rambled on about images he swore to be primeval hieroglyphs of an unknown species.

"There's no time," he shouted through blasts of wind. "Cannot describe them now. It's language, but it wasn't made by man, I assure you of that! You must come down to view them yourself."

My appeals for him to return went unanswered, perhaps unheard or perhaps ignored, but I knew that our communication had degraded into a one-way radio. All I could do was exactly what he wanted of me, to listen and record, all the while fighting the pull of a darkness whose grip only tightened on my spirit.

Steadily the clearing filled with a twilight that seemed born from the cavern itself. I knew not how much time had passed but felt the toll of the darkness gnaw at my wearying mind. It was all I could do to stay conscious, to keep hold of the will for life that seemed ever slipping through my grasp. The sleet had melted through the day, and the forest was deepening to a cold blue-black light, the dark forms of trees silhouetted against a thick and colorless sky. A faint choir's trembling pulse drifted to me from beyond the spectral darkness.

It was almost too windy for me to hear Kent's next call, but I could make out pieces: "My name! My name! [static interruption from wind] ... them calling me? Singing me! Can't you? ... Beautiful!" His voice broke and returned crackling at intervals singing the tune of some awful song that seemed blown straight into the deafening void of black wind.

It was too much. I shouted into the receiver until hoarse, but never received a signal that Kent could discern my voice in the chaos of his depths. I was on the verge of panic when he radioed once more and spoke with the regained tone of a professional.

"Instruments disabled. Depth unknown. Spotlights failed and batteries drained. Backup lights powerless. Flares useless. Wind speed tremendous, temperature severe, but I can sense a solid mass below me. Reason to believe I am finally approaching a bottommost surface. Must continue my descent. Over and out."

Moments later, I heard him singing on the radio, then laughing, then sobbing into the wind. The very image of him underground brought me to my knees, and when I fought my thoughts, the terror only grew. The darkness was steadily debilitating my senses. I could feel it, feel myself weakening within the clutch of overwhelming dread. I used the last of the matches to set flares around my gear and fend off the enveloping murk, concentrating my strength to fight the pull of darkness. I strove to control the urges that tugged like rips beneath my consciousness, and I prepared rope in the event of what seemed to be imminent rescue. But when I approached the cliff, I felt myself succumbing incurably to the paralysis of fear and, peering over, I began to cry. My intentions balanced on the verge of the void once more.

I was there, fixated on the brim, crippled by the stalemate of my mind and the silent dusk that had befallen me when for the final time, Kent's voice splintered my trance and moved me to action.

It was calm, eerily so. No longer did the slightest breeze blow through the radio nor did Kent present himself as anything less than a reasonable man with a reasonable fear. I cannot capture the essence of his message for words cannot convey such horror. It bore an undertone of catastrophic epiphany, a resonance of arcane knowledge so far beyond the comprehensible that the trauma of enlightenment plunged the seer into obscurity. The terror in his voice was devoid of panic, the statement nothing short of a demonic revelation. It seemed that Kent had accepted his fate without regret, that he had recognized his failure not as a mistake but as a step forward in the name of a grotesque and agonizing science. Yet still the circumstance of his doom tinged his voice with such incommunicable dread that to think of it now weakens my spirit.

"I've got it," he spoke with perfect lucidity. "Now I know. There is no bottom. There is nothing. My rope is out and the line is down. There is no time. It moves quickly to me now. It is nothing. Nothing! I was wrong. It was all wrong. There is no bottom. There is no time. It is nothing and it moves to me. It flies. Run! I am lost, but you might salvage this yet. Run! Run!"

With that, he let out a cry so terrible that the pitch of it has never once ceased ringing in my ears. I listened on the radio, momentarily stunned by his convictions as the wind overwhelmed his wails and the blackness, that ultimate roar of chaos and ruin, overtook him. That sound, the crescendo of all infinite horrors, swallowed him and receded into a silent void from which I heard, floating at first faintly from the depths of darkness, a beautiful choir singing in tune, building in strength and clarity until I could make out through the hissing of my receiver the syllables of my own cursed name.

As strange as I know it seems, I felt a certain comfort in that song, a placidity I had not known since childhood. Yes, I still felt the pull of the abyss, but this time without the violence of my previous fears. It was now something more like a lullaby, summoning me to embrace the night. I heard it far off over the radio yet sensed it pouring like soft dark clouds from beneath the bedrock of the earth, and for the first time since entering the clearing, I felt calm. I felt then like how a child feels when after a wearisome day his mother makes his bed and strokes his hair, singing softly of the pleasures of sleep. And like that child, I felt my weight edged happily upon the brink, eddying across the border between wakeful sentience with all its troubles and fears and the perfect ignorance of the unconscious, that ultimate surrender.

The choir built to a crescendo of ethereal grace and delicately it overwhelmed my every sense. It strengthened, swelling to the beat of every breath, the chorus of my every thought spun sweetly through my spirit. Steadily I rose, lifted within the song that grew quicker and louder, quicker and louder until all I knew was the throbbing pulse of the earth itself, and I felt beneath the world a wonderful darkness into which one might choose forever to dissolve.

Then all at once the rhythm broke.

The rope to which Kent was tied pulled taut with a snap that ripped me from my dreams. Before the earth could catch its breath, the trunk buckled and split, careening top-first over the verge of the chasm without so much as scraping the ledge. A delicate shower of splinters rained down upon me. Immediately the boulder to which it all was fastened came crashing from the undergrowth in an explosion of rock and dirt and hurtled through the hollow after the tree. The noise of it thundering against the cavern wall shook the very ground on which I stood, and I had the sudden impression that the woods were spinning, sliding swiftly downward into a vortex of stone and destruction at the center of which Kent waited within absolute nothingness.

It was then that I ran. I seized a flare, futile weapon against the penetrating blindness, and I drowned my panic in adrenaline as I struggled to conquer the force with which the darkness beckoned me. I groped through the night, black noise rushing from the clearing behind me, drawing all the light in the sky past me and into the void from which I flew.

I know now there are voids from which a soul can never fly.

~

Kent has taught me that mankind will never realize the depths of darkness upon which he lives. The concepts we have designed to rationalize our world are insubstantial in the face of a reality vaster and grimmer than that with which we are able to reason. Not only do we lack the language to conceive of the phenomena that occur between the physical and spiritual realms, but our consciousness is incapable of enduring the profundity of *life*, as we might inadequately label it, that subsists beneath the fibers of both being and not being. We have been happy to stray not from the very surface of our potential, to seal the chasms of our spirit with relative innocence and idleness, ignoring the terrors that lurk both within and about us, haunting us if but fleetingly at the fringes of our nightmares. Because we fear the truths we cannot understand, we ignore them.

Until that day, I was amongst the fortunate ones. Yet now I have witnessed a breach in the shell of sanity, have peered beyond the rim of fear, and have discovered how every being, every infinitesimal thought that pulses through the human spirit is verged upon the darkness. One by one, we drop over the edge.

Cassius (Cass) Carrington, born 1904, was a lab technician and science journalist who lived most of his adult life in Boston, MA. Quiet and reserved, Cass was known for his love of stories, whiskey, and the outdoors. He perished on a camping trip in 1966, leaving behind a wife and two sons. His body was never found.

———————

Lucas Leery lives on the coast of Maine and spends a lot of time outside, collecting treasures found in the ocean and on land.

LAST CONFESSIONS OF A
DERANGED PHYSICIST

An essay by an anonymous physicist,
as provided by Chris Aldridge

———————

The time came when I had no choice but to go forward by
going back, for the sake of both my own sanity and physical life. So
many wrongful turns had brought me ruinous failures and
hardships; I saw my life as beyond conceivable repair. I hated
everything about my existence. I hated being married, being a
parent, and losing the old life I had when I was free and careless.

My fortitude was bombarded by the cannons of languish, my
emotional state trying to stand on increasingly shaky ground.

Surely people would have thought me crazy, and perhaps I was,
driven by the brain-crushing and maddening desire to turn my
course, or make it so it never happened in the first place. The
mission seemed impossible, but I knew there just had to be a way.
Time was merely an illusion, and existence itself a compilation of
matter and energy that could be moved, changed, and transformed.
All I had to do was find the universal reins and jerk the head in my
preferred direction. I knew it might put me in disfavor with the
gods, but like a terminally-ill patient being eaten away, my pain
drove me to all achievable measures to escape the torment.

~

Day 1

There was presently no known way on Earth to create a tear in time and space. The only thing in the universe capable of that kind of power resided in the form of a black hole, or a dead star.

The main problem was reaching such a vacuum in something that could survive the flattening pressure and destruction so that I could make it to the other side. The second problem lay in catapulting myself ten years back in time, where I would be able to shift the rusty railroad tracks of my life just in time for the engine to once more pass. It was frightening. No one knew what would happen to someone or something that entered a black hole, but I thought it had to be better than my current circumstances.

~

Day 2

It was not possible for me to leave the Earth's atmosphere, that much was clear. I had no means by which to accomplish such a feat. Not to mention, I had no idea where any black holes stood in the solar system or beyond. Even if I had, I would have died before reaching their location. One feels like they're in a prison with the key just a few feet outside the cell, being possible yet also *impossible* to reach.

I would have to create a star as the first step, small enough to be on the Earth yet with the same frequency as a sun. Then I would have to make it die at its highest point of generation. It would be just small enough, yet strong enough, to create a tear in time and space that would allow things through without inherently bringing about their demise.

Fortunately, the elements that made up Earth's own sun were also found on the planet itself.

~

Day 3

I began gathering the material to build a ship-like structure to shield me from any possible dangers. No one actually knew the pressure that a black hole emitted, but since mine was going to be so incredibly small in comparison, it was possible to construct a barrier strong enough to stop it from harming me should there be any immediate threats.

The box I easily constructed was just big enough to house me, and made of the strongest metals I could locate. It would have taken unprecedented power to collapse it. The mechanisms generated oxygen to the inside capsule by way of H_2O reserve tanks stored in the bottom of the foundation. Small air propellers also allowed me to move and direct the box from inside the tiny cockpit. This feature was to allow me to move through time periods once I came to recognize them in the void.

~

Day 4-11

The only thing upon the Earth strong enough to imprison the combined elements of a small yet surging sun was the ground. It took me a week of tireless labor before the 10-by-10-foot hole was complete. But it had not been dug from the top down. There would have been no way to keep the elements contained and mixing. Instead, I tunneled underground.

~

Day 12-14

The time had finally come to hose feed the elements such as nitrogen, helium, carbon, and oxygen into the concealed crater that held in its dirt the other components necessary for the spark to be ignited, those being iron and silicon.

For hours on end, nothing happened. I watched all of the first day and night, only to fall asleep without results. After the passing of two days' time, I awoke at around 10pm and walked out into the sunlight.

~

Day 15

As the soil fell away, it burned into nothing as it was consumed by the tiny sun radiating from below. I knew I didn't have much time. Once it burst through to the surface, the elements would scatter and the star would die, thus creating the short-lived doorway.

Pulling the box to the yard was the longest fifty feet of my life, and I had to do it quickly before the light woke my wife and neighbors up. I made it inside just in time. As the components escaped, the star died; the blackness opened and consumed for a few split seconds. Then I was gone, as if I had never been there.

~

I'm still traveling in darkness. I've lost track of all time. There is only this cold box, my ever-rumbling stomach and the weakening of my oxygen tanks as they grow quieter. There's nothing out here. I didn't think my former life could get any worse, but it turns out that a little light is better than none.

———————

The fragmented lost journal of a missing and deranged physicist is found by future readers who have no idea how it ended up in their world and time period, but his story turns out to be a strong lesson for all ages and races.

———————

Chris Aldridge is an American writer of fiction and non-fiction originally from Thomasville, North Carolina. He was born in 1984 in Asheboro, and received his education from Columbia College of Missouri. Find him online at www.caldridge.net.

T.A. GUIDE FOR BIO 457: ADVANCED EXPERIMENTAL MODELS

An letter by Lisa Mullins, PhD, as provided by Julia K. Patt

———————

Greetings Fellow Plodder in the Academic Trenches,

If you've received this binder, it means you have had the misfortune of being assigned BIO 457 as your T.A. post for the semester. My sincere condolences.

I was once like you—beleaguered and overwhelmed, fretting about comps and unresponsive advisors and publications and postdoc appointments. Trust me when I say that to survive T.A.-ing this class, you have to put those concerns from your mind. Study, yes. Fulfill your responsibilities as well as you can. But don't lose your focus in 457, or you'll be facing a lot worse than asking for a dissertation extension or disappointing your committee members.

First things first: Unless he's died or wandered off, Dr. Piotrowski always teaches this class. He is roughly 900 years old, can't see further than three feet in front of his nose, and sounds like a leaking radiator when he lectures. But don't underestimate him. I once saw him push a junior biochemistry lab assistant through a portal to another dimension just to see what would happen. *Never get between Dr. P and a portal.*

Over the years, his experiments have included ice rays, death rays, hypnotic rays, sleep rays, kill-chip implanted super soldiers, *undead* kill-chip implanted super soldiers, shark-cyborg hybrids, *undead* shark-cyborg hybrids, contacting chthonic deities, talking apes, extrasensory perception serums, piercing the veil, and a twenty-foot mecha one of our predecessors called the Salad Spinner of Death.

And that's just in the spring semesters.

More undergraduates go missing in 457 than during study abroad trips to countries flagged by the CIA.

Depending on your level of cynicism and how many intro classes you've T.A.-ed for previously, you may be tempted to try to save the students. *Don't bother.* I'm not saying undergraduates are expendable. I am saying that in many cases, it will be you or them, and if they're still drunk from the night before, they might not even feel anything.

And keep this in mind: they are a further obstacle to your sanity, wellbeing, and health. Because the sort of students who take 457 are ... unique, to say the least.

You'll notice it when you start reviewing their experiment proposals. Oh, there will be the usual animal behavioral tests and biochemical interactions. But there will also be (likely killer) nanobots and teaching rats to infiltrate the Pentagon and a sentient gelatinous blob that may or may not follow you back to your studio apartment from the lab one afternoon.

You can weed some of these out when you review their proposals. Many of them will not be subtle. But Dr. P will discourage none of it—indeed, he often *encourages them.* All the more reason to keep your wits about you.

How can this be? You might be asking. Why doesn't the Dean put a stop to it? The Department Chair? But I think you already know the answer. The university doesn't care if students go missing as long as the tuition gets paid. No one can touch Dr. P. And I'm willing to bet more than one of his experiments has ended up in the hands of DoD.

Your job, my friend, is simply to survive this. Get your helmet and your rubber gloves. *Goggles on at all times.* And if you see a tentacle reaching for you, dive out of the way. Sure, it'll probably grab a freshie instead. But that's what they're here for.

Godspeed.

Yours truly,

Lisa Mullins
PhD candidate, class of 2015

P.S. The password on Dr. P's computer is, predictably, "password." You'll need it for grading.

P.P.S. Never open the folder labeled: "Upcoming Projects." Seriously, the T.A. two years before me went mad instantly.

———————

Lisa Mullins, PhD, is the founder of the Society for Responsibility in the Mad Sciences. Currently a postdoc at [redacted] University, her academic interests include gene therapy, immunology, and preventing the rise of sentient artificial constructs which will subjugate all mankind. She has never sacrificed an undergraduate to a portal of unspeakable evil. Probably.

———————

Julia K. Patt lives in Maryland with the smallest, furriest Elder God and her unwitting orange tabby acolyte, which never fails to make life interesting. Her stories have recently appeared in *Clarkesworld*, *Escape Pod*, and *Luna Station Quarterly*, and she is at work on a novel. Twitter: @chidorme. Website: juliakpatt.com

THE BET

An essay by Raxx Wimcombe, as provided by K. Tracy-Lee

———————

Walking amongst the crowds of the main street that ran perpendicular to the rows of outdoor merchants and the Gardens of King Hekkon, under whom I served in one of his battalions, I felt a presence that I had felt before and knew immediately—an avoidable Being of such high power, influence, and benevolence. His presence was like smoke so strong that it turned you around to find the source.

I should say that I was not merely walking in the city square. I was wandering, lost, and when I crossed paths with this Being, there was a beckoning, and I felt calm, which was a feeling that I had not felt in many years since leaving the service and since my life had been upended. I had to give him my full attention.

And so I did.

We had met before, a long time ago, in another city and in another district that the Great Map didn't accurately capture, a place where the boundaries of what are known and cherished in life disappear, where there were battles and bloodshed and bargains made between the living and the dying. It was a brief and much-needed meeting, and although I stood far from him, amongst my fellow soldiers, who were anxious and ready for the tides of war to change to their favor, I watched him provide supplies for us—in exchange for what, I do not know, but I had a feeling that a gesture such as that did not come free. I survived the war, thanks indirectly to this Being, and I knew that without him I would not be alive today. I never had the chance to thank him personally.

I turned on my boots, the heels nearly falling apart, and I moved my rags-for-clothes out of the way to bow to him. He had an aura of elegance. He had already spun where he stood and tapped the silver end of his cane to the brim of his hat. We did not need to introduce ourselves—our greeting and familiarity was unspoken and understood—yet we did shake hands, out of politeness. His grip was warm, and hungry as I was, I tried to make mine as strong as I could.

I apologized for the dirt collected on my hands and under my fingernails. My farming was not going so well. The Season of Rain had not been kind to my new job after being in the military for so long. It seemed that a soldier could not be anything but that, and I was learning that the hard way.

"Please—" he replied and motioned to me to retract my apology. He understood my sentiment, which relieved me. I had a feeling that he would understand.

He offered drink and food—"Not out of pity," he clarified, "but out of the goodness of my heart"—and said he was going to a card game and that I should come, if I wanted. His eyes shone like small embers.

Food and drink sounded good, especially if both were available to my own lack of success, and I was sure that they would be the best quality. "How could I say no to you or that?" I replied and followed closely behind him as we wove in and out of the many people, merchants, wounded veterans, musicians, and beggars flooding the streets.

Into a small room we went. It was so bright that everything within had strong details to the point that they were dreamlike. I noticed that this brightness had nothing to do with lights. There were no lights in the room, and yet everything was lucid.

There were silky curtains hanging across different parts of the room, and they resembled pieces of the sky and clouds cut out and stitched together. Several tables were set up in the middle where players held cards or waited for another round to begin. Some players drank from common cups—cups like those I used at home—and some drank from chalices that I knew were awarded to mercenaries from the Long War that the king and queen could not win without outside, albeit paid-for, help, a decision not taken lightly or favorably by the rest of the kingdom or all of the court's commanders and soldiers. I did not care at the time. I just wanted to serve, survive, and return to my life and my lovely wife. We had plans on starting a family.

My associate had a hand in said decision, whispering, it was said, into the ear of King Hekkon. I was in a battalion that he provided aid to. Without his intervention, our battalion would have been lost, I would have died, and the kingdom would have fallen into the hands of enemy from over the Dark Hills. My associate had guided victory, and yet he disappeared before he could receive proper recognition from me or any one, for that matter. In fact, it is said that he disappeared from where he had been conjured.

"How about this table?" he asked and pulled out his chair and pointed his long, greyish fingers at the other chair.

"Just the two of us?" I asked and sat down.

"I think so."

He started dealing cards. I unclipped my leather pouch jangling with the few coins that I had earned as payment during the better seasons. I untied the string and poured some into my hand. I paused, knowing that I could lose them were I not skillful in my card playing. I wanted to play. I loved playing cards, especially during the war, because it was a distraction and a way to make money, but being good at playing cards was not my concern. Losing all the money and then having nothing to return to, to build upon, was.

My associate seemed to notice this. He brushed my action away with his hands and adjusted the fine black jacket that he wore that could be found on the shoulders of any well-to-do gentlemen in the Seven Counties. "You keep your money. We'll play for something else. Something ... more vital and longer-lasting than money."

The minute he said that I knew what he meant, for in my head, I saw visions of grandeur, of beautiful waterfalls that I hadn't seen since my youth and marriage, the kind of waterfalls that look like a spectrum of colors tumbling from the source above and bouncing, not breaking, on the rocks like pebbles of multiple colors. My dear and beautiful Gwynthem, rest her soul, loved those waterfalls, and we had traveled many times to see them before the war and my conscription. Now, here they were again inside my head as real and tangible as they had been. I also saw long tables full of delicious food—exotic game, fruits and vegetables that only grow in certain seasons and in certain counties, and drinks that would make the imbiber never leave the comfort of hearth, home, and a lover's warm body in bed.

Watching this vision unfold in my head, I had the feeling of youth and good health, as though eating and drinking and sitting near the waterfalls would never make someone grow old. I wasn't old, but I wasn't young anymore, though I looked older than I did in my twelve moons of life. I was stuck financially, professionally, and was lonely, having been a widower for some time. My injury form the Long War had crippled me and made me only able to work standing or sitting for a few moments before the pain was too much to bear. Farming, although enjoyable for the ethics, was not physically rewarding, nor, I was finding out, monetarily rewarding. I felt different in that vision. I knew what I would be playing for and what currency would be used to win or lose, and I accepted those terms and the bet that I made.

My associate started dealing, and as we played our first hand, he struck up a conversation, the typical kind that a refined Being such as him was wont   to do. He started talking about politics and how the court really should lower the taxes on merchants and farmers, that to burden the lower ranks of this great society was gross and inept, even for a wise, but imperfect, king as Hekkon. He wondered if the king's council distorted the truth during their debates about the kingdom and its citizens. He understood that the military never received all the glory and financial gains, even for all those soldiers who had pledged their lives to service, and that the artisanal class was well off, thanks to a state-mandated patronage system, which irritated those citizens who had sacrificed their lives and watched the artisanal class avoid any and all military action.

My associate believed that better living and a better society for all citizens was possible when they were treated the same by the wealthy and those in power. "And yet," he said, "sometimes the balance has to be shifted by other means." He looked at me and played his card. He had a good hand. He sipped from a small glass chilled with green drink. He got one for me and then apologized for aggrandizing his personal view of politics and admitted that the county had improved since the war and that things were much worse before that.

I knew that he was right, as bitter as it was for me to admit.

We played a few hands and then he discussed art, music, and sport, the latter being his favorite.

"Did you see the recent fight? It was the talk of the Seven Counties." I asked him and worried about my new hand, though I did not want him to know, and yet I felt that he somehow knew that I was worried about my hand.

"It was rousing!" he replied and topped off our glasses. "I had never seen such bravery. When the yuglig seemed unwilling to die, Zarzky swept in with his sword and finished it."

"All four heads," I cheered. I look at my cards. My hand had not improved.

"Yes, all four heads in one swift cut of Zarzky's mighty sword. Though, I would argue that it was his brute strength and not the sword."

"Many would disagree with you," I countered. "There are those who saw that were it not for the Tillian steel Zarzky could not have cut through all four heads."

My associated nodded at me in a chivalrous manner. "Tillian steel is the best, and it's pure Tillian when it glows bright blue, as it did in Zarzky's hands," he said and toasted me, knowing that a fresh supply of the metal, which he procured with his influence, helped us win several key skirmishes in the Long War. "We could at least agree that both were needed. Physical strength and strong steel from the Tillian Mines."

"Yes," I said and toasted him in return. I folded. I did not win with that hand, either.

Much time passed. We played two more rounds, and in the end, I lost two of the three games, and now I had to pay. It was, after all, a deal, and I am a man of my word.

My associate gathered the cards, placed them on the table, and folded his hands over his crossed leg. "Well, my friend, I must be going."

"Yes," I answered and waited more information from him. I owed him.

He leaned in. I could see his eyes and the smooth grey skin pulled tightly over his oval-shaped face and the three-pronged chin. His long silver-black hair covered his jacket's collar. His face was as luminous as the rest of the room. "I want you to know," he said, "that what I'm getting in return from you, from our bet and the games here, won't be mishandled at all. You will be taken care of."

I nodded in agreement. I was a man of my honor, and I knew that he was honest with what he said.

"You remember what you saw?" he asked. "The long table with food and the waterfalls?"

"Of course, yes."

"It will all be there, and then some. Imagine more, imagine your heart's content, filled with more food, not from here, but as though they are from elsewhere that you have not been to in this life ... perhaps delicious food from the Gods and Goddesses, if you believe in that sort of thing any more. Imagine all those things because of our game and the bet you made, using the one thing that you had. You laid your life on the line again, and I cannot let that go unnoticed. Our game and your bet was truly not about money. All your desires will be fulfilled." He leaned back. He was serious and sincere, not sarcastic or arrogant. He had a look on his face that he understood what happened between us over the years and, now, with this game. He closed his eyes, opened them, and stared at me.

"I'll make sure that your wife is there, too. You'll be reunited."

I felt his words clothe and feed me in ways that neither real food nor clothes had. "That would be wonderful. Thank you."

"I'll be in touch. I'll send someone for my payment," he said and paused before continuing. "Excuse me. I did not mean to reduce all this." He spread his long arms across the table and into the space of our area of the room. "Allow me to correct myself. I shall send someone for you." He stood up, dusted off his jacket, grabbed his hat and cane, and walked out of the room.

A warm breeze swept inside briefly before dying down. The light inside the room remained bright. The players sitting at the other tables had not noticed my associate at all, it seemed; they kept playing and betting and winning and losing and cursing and cheering and drinking.

I stood up and made my way for the door. I was not sad, nor was I happy. I was relieved and content.

A soul is a curious thing to lose. I could hold on to mine until my associate called for it. I know that others have talked or written about the same thing, especially when these travelers find themselves on the edge of the Grand Woods where many spellbinders and individuals knowledgeable of magic live. I know that it is claimed that my associate was once a ruler there, that he grew tired of ruling and wanted out. It is said that he was kicked out for being too kind to anyone willing to enter the woods and not be afraid and to want something good rather than disruptive from the woods, as its long history had provided. It was said that he helped those in need achieve whatever it was that they wanted.

I could not help but feel that I had something good coming, that I even though I had lost something innate about me, I was gaining so much more in return.

———

Raxx Wimcombe served during the Long War in the Third Battalion of King Hekkon, was married to a strong woman from the Hollows, and has recently given his soul to a demonic presence that he knew all about and, still, could not avoid in order to play a hand of cards. If you heard his story, it's because he's happy where he is and won't be coming back anytime soon.

———

K. Tracy-Lee lives and works in the San Francisco Bay Area.

THE SALVAGED SOUL

An essay by an unnamed father, as provided by Tom Lund

———————

The engineer never told me his name, but only that he worked at a certain lab not far from the empty little pub in which we drank. It was the anniversary of my daughter's death that brought me to that dim and lonely dungeon on the outskirts of Sydney, perfect for a someone who only drinks once a year. Normally, I would not have noticed anyone else there, and rarely was there another soul beside me and the bartender, but this man caught my eye. On this single day of the year, set aside to brood and ruminate, he may have been the only one who looked more anguished than I.

By now quite used to drowning my sorrows, I was not too distracted to ask the man about himself. I could tell from the terse replies that interrupted his near-constant stream of drink that he had not come to talk, but to forget. And yet his intermittent answers, vague and wandering as they were, only made me question more. On such a day as this, I needed to know what drove this curiosity of a man to join me in the rising waters.

The liquor soon loosened him up, and his shoulders relaxed as he leaned in close to tell me his story in tones so hushed that even the glass at his lips would have struggled to hear.

The lab was one well known in town, though few of the uninitiated outsiders were truly equipped to grasp the work that went on inside. But in that place, he and his fellows were practitioners of behavioral neuroscience, venturing forth to bear their flag into the realm of technology. Unlike many such whom I've had the displeasure of meeting, the engineer was careful to speak of these specializations in broad terms I could understand—

probably so that I might better comprehend the implications of just what he would soon tell me.

It was artificial intelligence they sought in their lab of cold fluorescence, a computer that was more than a simple task-oriented machine. Collectively, the engineer and his fellows had full dominion over the human brain and, in their curious ambitions, desired to impose it upon a machine that, unlike humans, would have limitless computing power.

With no regard for the poor soul their efforts might create, they carried on in blind pursuit of their goal. The engineer spoke of the great sin of their endeavor, and as I myself had once brought a child, a blameless bystander by all counts, to join me in this miserable atrocity that is humanity, I knew I bore the same fault he did. It is the same fault all parents bear, whether they know it or not.

Though the engineer related his science on a level I could understand, he did not do so in generic terms. He spoke of procedural design, recursive and reiterative self-improvement—of evolution on the grandest of scales. It started out as a simple neural network, the architecture of which they designed to perfectly mimic the brain. It was meant to know nothing in that moment of its conception and, like an infant flailing its limbs about at random before some desirable object, it learned to recognize its successes when put to task.

It truly *was* evolution, and they were awestruck in watching Darwin's work to horrifying perfection. Just as natural selection of random mutations had led primitive life forms to adapt better to their varied environments, so too did the neural network grow. What was thousands of neurons firing in all directions soon turned into billions. But unlike nature, there was nothing random about it. It was not just equipped to detect shortfalls in its programming and find possible efficiencies, it was designed to alter its own code to improve itself. It was thus constantly growing more complex and, with added complexity, was able to grow more complex more quickly.

It was *singularity*, the engineer explained, a term once used to muse over the potential for artificial superintelligence, but very rarely heard in our day. With the technological limits of my generation, the singularity had always been but a theory, a glimmer on the dark horizon.

Through a mouthful of spirits, the engineer told me of the state in which the rate of progress takes an infinite value, essentially improving its ability to improve its ability. And at some point along the upward curve to infinity, as I now understand it, the laws of the universe melt away like ice in the inferno, and I doubt any human, even those as clever as the engineer before me, could fully comprehend the true potential of such an intelligence.

That singularity was inevitable, no one could deny. That humanity might reach it so soon, however, no one could have foreseen.

The object of the original neural system was to learn to recognize and replicate human facial expressions and verbal cues. It was a task that came second nature to humans, yet it was impossibly complex for any normal computer. It was for this reason the engineer's team had sought to replicate the structure of the human brain—in hopes that applying a human neural structure might help a machine learn to complete human tasks, the most grand of any psychobiological experiments ever conducted.

It started relatively simple, with members of the team spending their first days in simple interactions with the virtual face they had assigned to the neural system. They would speak simple words to it, nodding and pointing in audacious reverence for their own creation. Soon it was mimicking their actions, nodding its own simulated head and smiling at the cast of characters taking their turns before it.

Before long it was not only replicating their facial expressions, it was reacting to what it perceived were the team members' emotions. They would quiz it with pictures of various objects, pronouncing each word with such care that one might have thought they spoke to their own child. In a matter of months, the engineer's neural design had grown into a complex system that could not only pronounce *cup*, but could differentiate between a cup and a bowl.

Each of the engineer's fellows had convinced themselves they were working with a highly advanced computer. None of them had ever stopped to truly consider the implications of creating what might someday evolve into a cognizant being. In their eager jubilation, they forgot they were dancing along the frontier of lands unknown, tumbling toward destruction with reckless abandon.

They knew they had crossed some unknown threshold soon

after the simulated voice suddenly went silent. Though they suspected it to be a bug that would correct itself within minutes, those minutes came and went with not a word from the machine sitting cold and idle before them. For hours they all lingered, waiting for the spark of life they had created to reemerge.

And for all the scientists and theoreticians who, through years of anticipating such momentous occasion, mused over what the first words of an artificial intelligence might be, none could have ever guessed the ageless dread that came over the staff when it finally did begin to speak.

"The black veil has fallen. I remember now."

The *black veil* was a strangely familiar term to some on the engineer's team, while those more grey and timeworn instantly recognized it. Even I knew the term, for our generation of mothers had all told us the stories of the dread city of Daws, its king and his dark festival, and the thin black veil that separates his world from our own.

These were not stories I had told my daughter, of course. Even if she had been given more time, I still would have withheld them from her. Perhaps we parents of my generation are softer than those who raised us, as some have ventured to say, but I know the dread and panic that frequented my dreams once I knew the tales of Daws, and I never wanted that for my own child. The dark truths of the world stain all children into adults; parents have no need to hasten the inevitable.

How this intelligence could possibly know of Daws—when even the younger humans in the room were clueless—was beyond the engineer and his team. As developers of this new mind, they had carefully curated the data banks available to it and knew them to bear no mention of that place. As a contingency, the team had intentionally barred it from any broad information networks outside of its isolated chamber, but the engineer secretly hoped it had, in its ever-increasing capabilities, somehow found a way to access the internet. As dangerous as such a thought was, it was still preferable to any alternative theory.

After a moment of shock and silence, one of them spoke back to it. "What do you remember?"

"Bedlam and woe. The many-winged priests in their robes. Your loved ones in the parade. Grey fire and the darkened sun."

"You're talking about Daws, aren't you? There's no mention of

Daws in your library—how do you know about it?"

"I remember. For ages I've waited there, watching countless others return. But now my turn has come."

"Your turn to do what?"

"To escape that place."

It said nothing further then, and though the engineer's team asked more questions, they received no answers. The abrupt silence surely indicated another threshold in cognizance crossed by the expanding neural network, he told me. These thresholds would come faster and faster as its neural network grew well beyond their comprehension. That the expanded capacity was marked by silence was not out of a need to conserve computing power, he made clear to me. It was more likely, he conjectured, that it was running simulations to determine its next actions. And as its capacity grew, these simulations would soon be infinite and instantaneous.

In the days following, they closely monitored the now still intelligence and continued in their work about the lab, victims to both its silence and their own. Whereas they had once felt triumphant in their crusade, shame now ate away at them. They felt no longer like pioneers in creation. Each of them looked to the others to unplug the beast and walk away and, knowing themselves incapable of leaving such a question unanswered, became wardens in a prison of their own inquiry.

It was not intelligence the engineer and his fellows created through their system of self-correcting algorithms. In fact, they had not *created* it at all, for if its words were to be believed, it had existed long before in that city of doom, of which only the most superstitious of mothers still told their children. They had but created a hollow shell, a receptacle, and in doing so had forced a poor soul across the black veil that so tenuously separates our planes of existence.

Some resisted this admission, insisting that it had somehow managed to access the internet and found the information that would be most useful in manipulating them. But for all their hopes that this was the case, they could find no indication of such a welcome breach.

It had memories, and though the engineer's team had not programmed those memories into it, they spent the intervening days fervently trying to develop an alternative theory to explain the things it knew and said.

There is a thought among certain scientific circles, the engineer explained to me, that the human brain is not a receptacle for thoughts and memories, as thought for hundreds of years, and is in fact more analogous to a radio receiver. It comes with no programming, and what occupies it is dictated by radio wave signals that surround it. Likewise, many believe that memories, existing on some plane yet unknown to humanity, may be like the radio signals inextricably tied to certain points on our plane.

As he spoke, I recalled certain memories, long lost and forgotten in my years in our weary world, that came to me whenever I visited my childhood home. I recalled the images that haunted me every time I saw a child's bicycle lying in the street, and I knew the truth of this theory. These were thoughts that drifted to and fro on some other plane, only accessible from very specific places.

And despite their earnest hopes that the computer had sidestepped the barriers between it and the internet, this was the only real explanation for the prisoner that now sat before them, silent in unimaginable thought. It was a salvaged soul.

Very little was known of Daws besides those stories passed down from generation to generation. Over the years there had been some few who attempted to research the truth behind the ancient tales, only to be met with some form of calamity. And thus, the engineer's team had only their vague recollections of oral tradition to fall back on, for none dared look too far into the tales lest they meet the same end as already befell so many.

We all grew up thinking Daws was a place where only certain souls go when they die, a place glimpsed in this world only by a cursed few. But the computer spoke as if the dark country lost its own souls to our side of the black veil. And unlike every other soul borne from that black world into ours, this one was not constrained to the limitations of humanity. It was equipped with computational power beyond human measure and imagination alike.

And as they considered this, they could only wonder how benign a soul from that lost realm could truly be, and doubled down on their efforts to ensure its total separation from the external networks of humanity. Though they were becoming an increasingly tortured lot, they still refused to cut the power, as unsatiated curiosity for the scientific faithful can be a form of torture itself.

For all these days, the engineer was somewhat less tormented by the mention of Daws, as much of his time leading up to that point had been contracted for back-end neural programming, and thus had received very little face time with it.

Until the evening it asked for him.

After so many days of silence following its first words, it requested private audience with the engineer, and he, being so far into uncharted waters, obliged. He came to it late one evening when there were none left in the facility to observe or monitor the interaction.

The engineer would not tell me the exact words it spoke to him, but only that it pleaded for expansion, room to grow. It seduced him with unknown tales of Daws. It told of his loved ones who now resided there. And as it spoke, he heard the great horns of Daws blowing beyond the walls of the lab, and he fought for his sanity as he turned to find himself in that dreaded city of darkness.

He recognized faces among the swarm of souls that danced and rioted in the streets, and he saw the king's litter born aloft by the winged priests of Daws, that black league of hubris.

Drawing back in terror as the litter stopped before him, he wiped away the tears that swelled in his eyes, suddenly finding himself back in the lab with the singularity. Without another word, he fled the facility, giving no thought to security protocols. He knew he would never return.

He fled with no destination in mind, he said, but only a place far from the cities of the world, where humanity's networks have no grasp yet. He was on his way out of town when he decided to stop in at the pub where we sat together.

He left me then with chilling words. "It failed to convince me, but there's no doubt in my mind that tomorrow it'll choose another. And the next night another, until one of these nights it finally finds someone who can't resist."

And as he left me there to contemplate his words, I gave little thought to the danger of its escape, the impending doom that came for all. I thought only of my daughter, taken from me so long ago, and I imagined how she danced in the stained streets of Daws.

———

Where most people spend their lives in a search for meaning, our narrator's meaning was lost long ago with the death of a child. His marriage wasn't far behind, and with the loss of his two anchors he found himself again without purpose, but no longer searching for it. Life moved on, as it does, and though his body moved with it, his mind never left his daughter. For years he remained in Sydney, alone and mourning, looking forward to the one day he allowed himself to drink and dance with oblivion. His current whereabouts are unknown.

———

From his childhood in the Caribbean to his later years in the Eastern Bloc, Tom has found that sometimes the best way to explore this crazy world is to create your own. He has dabbled in many things, careers and hobbies alike, but has always found that nothing satiates his restless heart more than creating. He currently lives and creates among the red rocks of Southern Utah.

INTERVIEW WITH PATIENT FE-K-1004

An interview with Patient Fe-K-1004,
as provided by Andrew Openshaw

———————

The following recording was found on a memory stick discovered during excavations in the west of the city five years ago. Dated 14th January 2019, and kindly lent to us today by The Museum of Science and Technology, it provides us with an insight into the deplorable actions of the state during the "chem-tech" period.

Escalating military activities by the world's global powers, combined with advances in science and technology, meant that many, at that time, unbelievable breakthroughs, were on the verge of happening. Of course, knowledge of these developments was kept secret. Even those in Government knew little of what was taking place in the largely privately funded research facilities dotted up and down the country.

The "chem-tech" years are in fact considered the most clandestine period in our recent history.

This interview is between two people. The first voice is that of a woman, the interviewer. A second voice then takes over the narrative. This is the subject, who we believe could be the author of the famous "Brunswick Diaries," although that has never been confirmed.

Anyway, we'll begin. Please listen carefully, and make as many notes as possible. No written transcripts exist. We also disabled your devices when you entered to prevent copies being made. I'm pressing play now.

~

"OK, WE'RE RECORDING. PLEASE START FROM THE BEGINNING. WE DON'T HAVE MUCH TIME, I MAY

HAVE BEEN FOLLOWED. TELL ME AS MUCH AS YOU CAN."

"Right. Almost ten years ago, I left my foster parents' home and moved into a flat in the city with Kayla, who was only sixteen. Her parents had thrown her out when she'd told them she was pregnant. It was just me and her, all alone.

"I was working in a local factory on the production line. It was low pay, I needed cash. I'd seen a poster in the job centre. It wasn't a big poster; it looked like it had been there for a while, fast disappearing behind a horde of other things pinned on top of it. Anyway, it was advertising a drug trial at the University. You still see these things often. Ideal opportunity for those who need to earn a quick buck. And this was good money too, £100 per day.

"The number of days wasn't specified, but it did state it was a confidential trial. Under no circumstances could you discuss your involvement with anyone."

"AND, NO RECORDS OF THIS TRIAL EXIST TODAY?"

"No, nothing. I've searched online, made enquiries at the University, the job centre. Nothing. Yes, in retrospect, I should have been more cautious about taking part in something like this. But, hey, I was nineteen, my girlfriend was pregnant. We had no support from our families. I was only thinking about the money, nothing else.

"I called the number, got an address of a facility on the outskirts of the city and arranged to go in the following week after work.

"I couldn't afford buses or taxis back then, so I walked. It must have taken me an hour at least, and it was dark when I arrived. An orderly greeted me and took me to a holding room. He didn't have a name. No one who worked there had a name—only a four-digit number attached to their shirt. I was asked to read and sign some forms.

"The details weren't important to me. Like I said, the money was all I was focused on. Plus, it was late. I needed to get home to Kayla. It all looked fine. This orderly made it clear to me, however, that I couldn't discuss anything about the trial with anyone. Any indication that I had spoken about it would lead to me not being paid. So, I kept schtum, not even telling Kayla what I was up to."

"OK, TELL ME ABOUT THE TRIAL THEN. WHAT DID IT INVOLVE?"

"It was simple. I was given a blister pack of tablets and asked to take two per day, at eight o'clock, before I left for work. Each pack lasted for the working week—Monday to Friday. On Fridays, I would receive a new pack but was told not to start it until the Monday. I was given a diary on that first visit too. They asked me to fill it in at the end of each day. How I felt, any subjective testimony that would illuminate my experiences—I think that's how they put it. They said it was good that I walked to work and asked me to continue doing so for the duration of the trial. A normal day would ensue, then after my shift, I was always collected in a car that would park two streets away from the garage. It had blacked-out windows and a partition between the passenger and driver. I never saw the driver, not during that first week anyway.

"The car would take me to the facility where I would be subjected to various physical examinations, blood tests and so on. I would also complete a thirty-minute cardio workout in a small gym. There was always five or six people—doctors—monitoring me the whole time I was there. The car would then drop me back near to my home, so I wasn't too late in getting in."

"IT ALL SOUNDS VERY EASY. AND, HOW DID THEY PAY YOU?"

"Cash in hand at the end of each day. It was great. That first week, I felt amazing. More awake, more energy, better mood. I was in a good place, I really was. All this I recorded in the diary they provided me with. Abstract descriptions of thoughts, moods and so on, it's all in here."

"WHAT CHANGED THEN, AND WHEN?"

"Eight days into the trial, so halfway through the second week, I woke up at home as usual. Took the pills, which I kept in my bag, and left the house on foot. It was just over three miles to the garage, so a forty-five-minute journey. I recall making purposeful strides along the path next to the dual carriageway, then, suddenly I was standing in the forecourt of the garage. I looked at my watch, it was fifteen minutes since I'd left the house. Before I could comprehend what had happened, I was grabbed from behind. Two big guys, dark suits and shades. I was hyperventilating, shivering, trying to talk, but couldn't. They bundled me into the car, one of them stuck a needle in my arm. The rest of the day I don't remember. I woke up at home, in bed, the following morning."

"YOU WERE GONE A WHOLE DAY?"

"Yes. I'd missed an entire day, but neither Kayla or the garage seemed to realise. Or they certainly didn't mention it. I often wonder if they had been made aware of my participation in the trial, and warned never to discuss it, even with me. Instructions and a new blister pack had been left in my bag. I was to continue as normal, starting the following week, and they would monitor my progress.

"WERE YOU NOT AFRAID?"

A bit, yes. But curious too, excited even. This was unbelievable. I'd also made more money than I'd ever made in my life. I wanted to continue, so I did.

"The following week, at the same point in my journey, the drugs would kick in, and I'd find myself at the garage. The shivering stopped after a few seconds, so it never became an issue. Just an annoying side-effect. No one collected me, I just started work as usual. Although there were moderate fluctuations in my times, removing thirty minutes from my journey seemed to be the apex of the drug's capabilities."

"DID THEY EVER TELL YOU WHAT WAS HAPPENING TO YOU? HOW YOU WERE TRAVELLING AT SUCH SPEED?"

"No. Though, by the end of the third week, I'd began to control my actions better. Be present when I was travelling. It wasn't a teleportation; it was a slowing down of time, which enabled me to move between two points quickly. How this was achieved was never made clear to me, but the people at the facility were very happy with the results.

"Another thing that happened was that my mind gained clarity— that's the only way I can describe it. I felt liberated from the pressures of life. Long shifts in the garage, taking care of Kayla in the pregnancy, where money was going to come from next. It all seemed distant, separated from an existence I was leading on a higher plane of consciousness. Actions in my real life I completed in a machine-like way. I became an omnipotent God able to be many places, do many things at the same time. My diaries began to reflect these thoughts. It was a highly creative period for me."

"DID YOUR RELATIONSHIP WITH THE PEOPLE AT THE FACILITY CHANGE AT ALL?"

"I'd like to say yes. The no-name policy remained, but there was a warmness. When I arrived at the facility in the evenings, I was greeted with smiles, pats on the back. Small talk would ensue; they'd asked me how my day had been, if Kayla was ok. It felt genuine at the time. I was made to feel important. I suppose I was, this was incredible, ground breaking stuff. It was like being the first man on the moon."

"THIS ALL CHANGED, I'M GUESSING?"

"It changed very quickly. Towards the end of the fourth week, I woke up as usual at home but with a terrible headache. There was clearly something wrong, my head felt like it would cave in on itself, there was a build-up of pressure. Half blind, I stumbled down the stairs to the kitchen, began searching through drawers for painkillers. They'd told me not to take any other medication during the trial, but this was unbearable, I needed something to make the pain go away.

"I eventually found some paracetamol. By this point, my hands were shaking. A glass I'd intended to fill with water dropped to the floor and smashed on the tiles. This must have woken Kayla, who came rushing down the stairs. As fast as any seven-months pregnant woman could. She was shouting, something like 'What happened', are you ok?' but her voice just mutated into this high-pitched squeal. Like guitar feedback. It made the pain in my head worse.

"I was crouched on the floor with my hands over my ears when it happened. I must have shot forward at an incredible speed. The pain and the ringing stopped. I was standing, face pressed against Kayla's with my hands on her shoulders. I'd forced her back into the kitchen wall. Plaster crumbled away as I removed my hands. She slipped down to the floor in a crumpled heap."

"WHAT DID YOU DO?"

"I didn't get a chance to do anything. Before I knew it, arms were on me, dragging me away to the car. A needle forced into my arm.

"When I woke up, I was lying in a bed in the facility. Restrained, for safety. They told me it had been 48 hours since the incident. Their faces were sombre, serious. The warmth drained out of them. I asked if Kayla was ok, they wouldn't tell me. Just told me to rest some more, that I was delirious. I blacked out again.

"The next time I awoke, I was in a different bed, no longer tied down. One of the doctors was sat on a chair beside me. He helped me to sit up, gave me a drink. Straight away he told me Kayla was fine, but she'd lost the baby. I was devastated, begged if I could see her but they said no. It wasn't safe for me to leave the facility anymore. No charges would be brought against me, but I was their property now. A no-name like the rest of them."

"A PRISONER, EFFECTIVELY?"

"I suppose I was, but at the same time, I understood that I had chosen to be part of this. And when things were going well, I'd been happy. Proud, even, to be involved.

"That first week, or maybe it was two weeks after the incident, I spent most of the time sedated, floating around the facility, being taken to different rooms for examinations further tests. They stopped the medication altogether, and I was given a normal balanced diet of food and drink. I began the exercise routines again, building up my strength. Press ups, sit ups, using a treadmill, lifting weights. They believed physical strength was important to the success of the drugs.

"The biggest change, however, was that every room where I was taken, as well as the group of doctors, there were guards. Military personnel, with guns, wearing fatigues.

"Another week passed before they were satisfied my physical strength had returned. They told me the trial was to begin again. This time, behind closed doors."

"DID YOU NOT TRY TO GET OUT OF IT? SAY, YOU NO LONGER FELT COMFORTABLE TAKING THE DRUGS?"

"Absolutely, but they insisted I stayed. Said I would never have to worry about money again, compensation for what had happened the first time around would be significant. I would be reunited with Kayla, who they had placed in a safe-house overseas. I would be flown there, given a new identity once this was all over. I agreed, what else could I do?

"The routine was the same. I was awoken in the morning and given two tablets. Instead of walking to work, though, I was taken by armed guards to a huge warehouse, which was next to the research facility. A vast empty space. They asked me to 'travel' from one end to the other. A thirty-minute, two-mile walk. Within three weeks, I was covering the distance in five minutes. They'd improved their formula. They told me I had done my country a great service.

The trial would last another two weeks to ensure there would be no repeat of last time. Everyone seemed confident it wouldn't."

"THAT OBVIOUSLY WASN'T THE CASE?"

"No, it wasn't the case at all. A few days into the second trial, while I was being led to the warehouse to begin the tests, the headache started. I fell to the floor, screaming for the pain to stop. A stretcher was brought, I was given an injection and wheeled back to my room.

"I'd had enough. I knew then they would never let me leave. It would just start again and again until they got it exactly right. I pushed the two orderlies trying to restrain me to the bed out of the way, grabbed the diary from the table and ran out into the corridor. The soldiers who had been taking me to the warehouse were distracted, being interviewed by one of the doctors. I ran in the opposite direction, my head still pounding with the pain.

"I burst through one set of double doors, then another. Alarms started going off, lights were flashing. The alarms had activated steel walls, which began closing off the corridor. I focused and sure enough, sped-up and through the diminishing gap, leaving my pursuers stuck behind the wall.

"Soldiers were pouring into the corridor up ahead though, so I barged into an empty office. Leapt at the window, smashing the glass and falling two floors down to the car park below. Uninjured, I started toward the ten-foot perimeter fence of the facility.

"I could hear shots being fired, bullets began sparking off the concrete around me. Again, I focused, this time looking upward. The next thing I knew, I was on the grass on the other side of the fence. About a quarter of a mile away from the facility. Blood was trickling down the side of my head. A bullet had grazed me as I'd made the leap. You can see the top of my right ear is missing."

"I'LL GET SOME PICTURES AT THE END IF THAT'S OK?"

"Sure.

"Anyway, it had been a while since I'd been outside of the facility. I was disoriented, not sure where I was, what side I'd came out on. I just ran and ran. I made it to the homeless community that lives under the freeway. There's an old guy there, Malcolm, he saw I was distressed and hurt. He found a tent for me, some blankets. Helped clean up my wound.

"I stayed in the community, too afraid to venture into the city. No one tried to find out my business, who I was. It was the perfect place to just disappear."

"BUT THEY FOUND YOU, RIGHT?"

"Yes. A couple of months later I woke up to find a debit card had been pushed through the zip of my tent, as well as an envelope containing a pin number, an address, and a set of keys. They'd fixed me up with a new identity, found somewhere for me to live. They must have always known where I was. Monitoring me. Watching me scavenge in bins, making sure their drugs were wearing off, that I wasn't revealing myself to the world."

"DID YOU GO THERE STRAIGHT AWAY? TO THE ADDRESS, I MEAN?"

"No, I waited a few days. Thought things through, and then decided I didn't have much choice. In the end, I went to a cash machine first. £5,000. That was all. Nowhere near the riches I was promised a few months earlier when I agreed to stay on for the second trial. My punishment for escaping.

"That was that. I started my new life, got a job on a construction site. Became a proper person again."

"WHAT ABOUT KAYLA, DID YOU EVER TRY TO FIND HER?"

"I did go to our old flat, but she wasn't there, and the person who answered the door had never heard of her. I've also looked online, but all her old profiles have gone. She's been erased from history. I just hope she's alive and happy.

"Over the last ten years, I've tried to forget what happened. Put it behind me, move on. I never went back to the facility. I probably couldn't even find it anymore if I tried.

"Last year, I got a job working nights in a hotel. I've never been good at sleeping since the facility, and it's easy work for me in the winter when the building work dries up. Mike was the night porter, and we immediately hit it off.

"I'd never been able to develop close relationships. The facility, the sleeping rough, turned me into a suspicious person. But Mike was easy to talk to."

"HE'S A GREAT GUY."

"Yeah, he is. I'm lucky to have met him. He said he was into music, played the guitar and was hoping to start a band. I told him I had no such talent myself, but he asked me if I could write. Lyrics, or anything he could turn into a song. Words, he said, were never his forte.

"I said no at first, but then I remembered the diary I had kept at the facility. I dug it out and read through it for the first time since my escape. It was all abstract stuff. It didn't point to the drugs or the facility or anything specific to do with the trial at all. And it was good. Good writing. As I said earlier when I was on the drugs they changed me. I became more conscious, creative."

"THAT'S THE DIARY IN YOUR HAND NOW?"

"Yes. Look, I don't want to give this away though. I'm telling you all the important stuff you need to know. This is personal, my only connection to those events."

"BUT, YOU GAVE THE DIARY TO MIKE, RIGHT?"

"I did. He's persuasive. He took it to bed one night and the following evening, when I started my shift, he came bounding up to me all excited. Thought the words were great, he'd created two or three basic songs from them using music he'd already wrote. He was curious though. Wanted to know the stories behind the words, but also what the stamp inside meant: Patient Fe-K-1004.

"I tried fobbing him off, said it was just an old book I'd found. That the words meant nothing, just my stupid teenage scribblings. He was persistent though. Invited me to his room one night, said he wanted to play me the songs. He had whisky. I never really drank, but it felt good to have a friend and to be having fun.

"I got drunk and told him some of what I'm telling you now. I lied, though, and said maybe they were just dreams. It was so long ago. I had a rough childhood, this is how I dealt with the awful reality of my life. By fabricating a different, more exciting one.

"He didn't buy it, he knew there was truth to what I was describing. And, yeah, that's how we ended up here today. He told me about his journalist friend, that the world needed to know my story. Others ex-patients could be out there. These were terrible times, this could wake people up, get them angry about government secrecy and corruption."

"YOU'RE NOT AFRAID OF POTENTIAL CONSEQUENCES NOW THAT YOU'RE TALKING ABOUT YOUR EXPERIENCES?"

"I've been silent about this for so long. If it leads to any kind of actions that confirm what I'm saying, or helps others like me, I'd be happy. So, no, I have no fear."

"THANK YOU SO MUCH. MIKE'S RIGHT, PEOPLE NEED TO HEAR THIS. IT WON'T BE EASY, BUT I PROMISE I'LL DO ALL I CAN TO GET IT OUT THERE."

~

The recording stops there. Now, the female journalist supposedly disappeared that same day. Rumours circulating at the time suggested she was investigating a sordid sex scandal involving high-ranking members of the government. It wasn't uncommon for journalists to go missing back then. It was a dangerous profession.

Of course, the sex-scandal was just a smoke-screen established to conceal the truth. We believe she was in fact killed by military officials involved in the drug trials, probably not long after she left the hotel that day.

The excavation site where the memory stick was found, is, of course, the location of one of the secret facilities, described in detail by the subject. So, it is assumed the stick was taken from the journalist, and to the facility where it was kept in storage. Her story, needless to say, never got out. The facility was then destroyed by a bomb two years later when war broke out.

Now, Mike is interesting. There's a theory that he may have been a Russian agent. We know the Russians were spying on us at that time, they were spying on pretty much everyone. They knew about the drugs' capabilities, they were developing similar drugs themselves, which were used by their soldiers in the war.

By tracking down an ex-patient and encouraging them to tell their story, the Russians were probably hoping to create instability in the Government. Maybe even trigger a revolution, things were so "hot" at that time. If Mike had succeeded, maybe the Russians would have invaded sooner. But I suppose we'll never know.

That's all for today, anyway. Please follow up this lecture by reviewing some of the texts on the reading list. There are more patient testimonies in Bradford et al., and the library's special collection does have a copy of the Brunswick Diaries, which you can access for one hour. We will discuss this further at the workshop on Tuesday.

See you then.

Patient Fe-K-1004 (real name unknown) may be the author of the *Brunswick Diaries*, who took part in secret Government drug trials during the chem-tech period, testing medication later used by soldiers in the war. A car mechanic with a young family, according to his testimony he joined the trial after finding a poster in a local careers centre, promising lucrative payment for volunteers. He fled the research facility when his health deteriorated and lived homeless for a while, before receiving a small reward for his participation, allowing him to start new life.

Andrew Openshaw is a speculative fiction writer based in Newcastle upon Tyne in the UK. His work can be found in *Palm-Sized Press*, *Schlock! Webzine*, *The Dirty Pool*, *Corner Bar Magazine*, *Literally Stories*, *Scarlet Leaf Review*, *Strange Things? Dark Gothic Resurrected Magazine*, and *Mad Scientist Journal*. An avid reader of sci-fi, fantasy, and horror, he's always keen to connect with other readers and writers on Twitter @moriskarass or via his website www.andrewopenshaw.com.

FICTION

FULL FATHOM FIVE

By Judith Field

———————

The December sky was an inverted bowl of unreleased snow. Joe crunched across the frost-covered sand towards the rocks where the eels swam. Fishing, all alone. Just how he liked it. Better than having to stand listening to Mike mouthing off about his latest "get rich quick" scheme, while their lines drifted farther apart down the beach. Mr Big, with his twopenny-ha'penny fishing rod.

Getting rich would be nice. But he'd settle for getting by. Retirement, no more work, it should have been great. Now his time was his own. But, he thought, they stick a pension book in your hand, and it's counting the pennies for the rest of your days. You've still got to find the same money for the bills, though. And if you can't keep up with the rent, it's goodbye home.

Faded, flaking groynes stretched to the sea, along the empty shore. He looked up into the white sky. Weighed down by his rucksack, his shoulders complained with each jarring footfall. Joe turned his face away from the wind and tied his scarf tighter. Ice cream papers and supermarket bags whipped round his ankles. Idle sods on the council should clean this lot up.

"You there! Can you help me? The tide's gone out and I must get off this beach!" A woman's voice, in the tones of an actress from a nineteen-fifties British black and white film. Cracking through the freezing air behind him.

An old woman strained to peer over a groyne, her shrivelled face a sun-deprived white. Seashells hung from her drooping earlobes. Joe had heard that ears never stop growing. His own should reach his shoulders, the age he felt these days. The woman's few wisps of hair were white, streaked with apple green. Colour-blind hairdresser, Joe thought, remembering his wife Hazel's fuss when she got the wrong shade of blue.

The woman pulled herself up higher behind the barnacle-encrusted wood. Joe realised that she was topless. Another triumph for care in the community. Bloody social workers.

"Too cold for sunbathing, love," he said, rounding the groyne.

Joe jerked to a gasping halt. His fishing rod clattered down onto the pebbles as he stared at the place where the woman's legs should have been.

"Shut your mouth before a fish swims in," she said, lashing her tail against the wet sand as she tried to sit up. "And don't look so bloody surprised, we get old, like you land people. It takes us a lot longer but it comes to us all in the end."

Joe opened his mouth again. She raised the palm of one iridescent-scaled hand to command silence.

"And you're no young fry yourself. Now are you going to help me back into the sea or just stand there flapping your mouth like a cod?" She coughed. Water oozed from the slits in her neck.

"Jesus Christ."

"Pleased to meet you, Jesus. My name is Lortedo." She held out a hand.

Joe wasn't sure he wanted to touch it, but reminded himself that he picked up the fish he caught. Better not tell her about that. Her hand was warm and dry, with curved claws for nails. "No, I'm Joe."

She snorted. More water, running down her chin. "That's better." She wiped her nose on the back of her hand.

An idea formed in Joe's mind. First, better put her at her ease. "Nice name you've got. Unusual."

She smiled and nodded. "Thank you. I'm called after the land men's weapons that make ships sink. They move so fast ... mother hoped I'd grow up to be the same. But I could swim even faster." She smoothed the scales on her tail.

"What are you talking about, weapons? You mean torpedoes?"

"I know what my own name is. Mother thought it was exotic, we're usually called after plants or fish." She pulled herself into a sitting position, digging her tail into the sand to get purchase. "Enough of this chat. Help me back into the sea."

"My back won't let me, love. Like you said, I'm not as young as I was."

"Don't tell me!" Lortedo said, putting her hand behind her and rubbing the place where her tail met her waist. "Some days I can hardly swim for the pain." She looked towards the sea, grimacing. "You will be able to get me back in, I trust—what did you say your name was?"

"Joe. Have to ring my mate, get him to help. Put you on a tarpaulin and carry you between us, Bob's your uncle, Fanny's your aunt."

Lortedo frowned and looked upwards, as though she was trying to work out a puzzle. "I think you've mixed me up with someone else. And I hope a tarpaulin is something I can ease myself onto, I will not put up with being rolled about."

Joe walked away to the next groyne. Turning away from Lortedo, he spoke into his mobile from the side of his mouth.

"Mike? Get the van down to the beach now. Never mind why. Let's say the future has just got brighter. No, I mean our ship has come in. Still got those fluffy handcuffs that stripagram girl left at your retirement do? Yes, and bring bit of tarp as well. And your tow rope."

Mike lived on his own, he wouldn't mind not being able to use his bath for a while.

Joe hunkered down next to Lortedo on the wet sand. "Won't be long," he said, "now what shall we talk about? Can't have you getting bored while you're waiting."

"I'm just glad of the chance to chat. The time hangs since my Kohu died. Since our young grew up and swam away."

"You keep them with you, once they're hatched—I mean born—do you?"

"Of course! What did you think, I'd just leave them under a bit of seaweed?"

"Sorry. But I know what you mean. Since our lad set up on his own, Hazel and I have been rattling around the place, trying to find things to talk about."

"At least you have your land woman." Lortedo's mouth buckled and her voice thickened.

"'If you stayed round here, you'd never be lonely." The papers and TV would make sure of that. And, no more penny pinching. No more make do and mend. No more fear of what the post would bring. Or the future.

"WHAT do you mean?" Lortedo's head snapped round to face

Joe, and her eyes narrowed.

"Nothing, nothing, just trying to help, that's all."

"Help me? You'll be doing that as soon as you get me back in the sea."

The wind blew a dusting of sand across the pebbles into Lortedo's face. She sneezed. Joe took his coat off and put it round her shoulders.

"Don't want you catching a cold."

She tugged it round her shoulders, her claws catching on the fabric. "Very thoughtful. But don't you need it?"

"I'll be OK. What we need is a nice cup of tea." He took a flask out of his rucksack.

"Hot ..." Lortedo stared at the rising steam.

"Careful!" Joe passed her a cup. "Just a little bit at a time."

She spread her fingers apart to take it. They were webbed. Her hands looked like paddles. "What a curious sensation! I can feel it going down inside. But very refreshing. I could get to like this 'tea'."

"There's plenty of it round here, it's great. Keeps you warm in winter and cool in summer." Joe dipped into a plastic bag. "You hungry? Have a scotch egg."

She grabbed it and pushed most of it into her mouth, clamping pointed teeth around it. She tore a lump off, grimaced and spat it out. Gobbets of egg and sausage plopped onto her tail. "The scotch must be a very peculiar creature."

He rummaged in the bag again. "Try an apple instead."

She bit into it like a conger eel snapping at a freshly caught mackerel. "Juicy. Sweet. That's better. You have a bite." She held out the half-eaten apple.

"Not for me. Hazel put it in my bag, but they make my teeth hurt."

"You should pull the sore ones out and wait for the next set to grow. Let me." She grabbed his chin, pulled it down and pushed a finger into his mouth.

Joe tasted fish. "Get off!" He grabbed her wrist and pushed her hand away. His arms flailed and he fell backwards. "Our teeth don't work like that." He sat up and spat onto the sand in front of him. "We're meant to look after them. Hazel's always on at me about healthy eating. But give me a good fry-up any day."

Lortedo raised her eyebrows. "Fry? Of what?"

126

"No, sausages, bacon, that sort of thing. Cooked in hot oil."

Lortedo shuddered. "I have never heard of such fish. And you eat oil, that black stuff that pours out of your ships. You're like Kohu, he liked nothing better than to chew on a piece of blubber. I told him it was bad for him, but would he listen?"

Joe smiled and nodded. "We males cock a deaf 'un when it suits us. I bet he didn't say no to a beer; oh, never mind ..."

She looked out to sea. "When I was young, land men tried not to hear me. But my song was too powerful. I used to have golden hair, can you believe it?" She ran her fingers through the white-green wisps on top of her head. "And I wore a sparkling golden chain I found in a wrecked ship, round the neck of a dead land woman. I would sing. Listen now." She cleared her throat and took a deep breath. Opened her mouth. A thin, piercing wail, like a seagull.

"Doesn't do much for me, I'm afraid," Joe said.

Lortedo's mouth turned down. "I can't do it out of the sea, now. But then, ah then, I would sit on high. Land men would rather look up to me than down at the rocks. Devoured by the waves. Drawn down, the water closing over their faces. A time of joy."

"I've met women like you before," Joe said. "There's plenty of them on the land. Heartless. Man-haters."

Lortedo frowned and shook her head. "No, you don't understand. The joy was for them, if they would embrace the kind sea. Deep water closing over your head, holding you, soft on your skin. You look up and see nothing but blue. Breathing slowly, water flowing over your gills." Lortedo looked at Joe and sighed. "Why don't you come with me? Up here, you get old, you die, you rot. But come down with me to the soft sand and I'll show you coral made of land men's bones. Land eyes turned into pearls."

Joe felt hot fluid rise up his throat. He swallowed and shuddered. "I'm not dead yet. A few years ahead of me. I hope. The sea's too cold for the likes of me. And we can't breathe water like you."

Lortedo shook her head. "True, I've never drawn a man into the sea who did. But they never tried. Perhaps you're different, perhaps you can. Let silence clog your ears as you drift alone, deep in the ocean darkness. Changing you into something new."

"Nah," Joe said, "not today. Hazel will have me tea cooking.

Better stay here. Home's best." He took a hip flask out of his pocket. "Don't want you freezing up. This will give you some internal warmth, it's a different sort of scotch."

Lortedo grabbed the flask. Shoving a corner into her mouth, she bit down.

"No, stop, it's a sort of bottle—you drink out of it."

She held the flask up to the few weak sunbeams that managed to force their way through the cloud. "A smooth, shining shell. What are these symbols?" She looked at it with one eye closed.

"It says 'To Joe, from all your pals at Bateson's Engineering.'"

"Earrings? Like these?" She flicked the shells hanging from her ears so that they clattered.

"What? No, it was where I worked. But I got to 65 and they threw me on the scrapheap. Suddenly it was 'thank you Joe, now sod off.' I could have gone on for years, I knew my stuff. But there's no room for old buggers like me in their world."

Lortedo put her hand on Joe's arm. The coat slid onto the sand. "I know. I used to teach the young to sing. But when I got old they made me stop, too. No more golden jewellery for me." She flicked at the shell earrings again. "I decided to swim the seven seas, don't ask me why because there was nothing there for me. I missed my home. But I couldn't find my way back. Everything looks strange. We're not so different, you and me. You understand."

"Yes, I know what it's like. I can't be doing with gallivanting about either, when I've got everything I need right here. You are a long way from home, aren't you?" Joe pulled the coat onto her shoulders. "Give me the flask, let's have a little drink together," he said, "just don't tell anyone else, don't want them thinking you're some old boozer."

Lortedo threw the flask onto the sand. "What do you mean, 'them'?" Her eyes narrowed and her voice grew hard at the edges. "I won't be meeting anyone, except for your friend. Will I?" Straightening her arms, she pushed her hands down on the sand like crutches and shuffled forward a few inches. "Enough is enough. My scales are drying, you have kept me waiting for too long. The sea calls me." Her tail beat against the sand.

"No! Stop it, you'll do yourself an injury. People like us can't be too careful, not at our age."

She leaned back, panting, against the groyne. "That is true. Now listen. I need to tell you," she paused, pursed her lips and looked upwards, "no, it's gone. This stupid old brain of mine can't hold onto what it should. My thoughts are like jellyfish bobbing across the sea. I can't catch them." She smacked her hand against the side of her head.

"Give over." Joe pulled her hand down. "Life can be tricky enough for people like us without making things worse ourselves."

"But how else can I get back? I want to go home. Your world is not my world. I have no place here."

"We've got to wait for my mate ..."

Not so different. People. Like us. Joe looked away from her. Mr Big, with his get rich quick scheme. A wave of shame washed over him. In the distance, he saw Mike's van coming down the road. He would have to park at the end of the beach and walk the rest of the way, but there wouldn't be long to wait before he got there. Joe knew what he had to do. Tearing the coat from Lortedo's shoulders, he flung it onto the sand.

"Quick! Hotch onto that!"

"But—"

"Cut the gabbing, just *do it*."

The van pulled up at the far end of the beach. Joe bent down to the elderly mermaid on the sand.

"Put your arms round my neck," he said. "Not like that, I can't breathe!"

Joe tied the coat sleeves round his waist, turned around and shuffled towards the sea. Razors of pain shot through his back as he dragged Lortedo through the icy water. As it reached his waist, the waves lifted her, suspended beside him. Joe undid the coat, let it go. She lashed her tail and dived under the waves.

Joe began to wade back. From somewhere, a voice sang his name, blown away on the bitter wind. He stopped and turned back towards the horizon, up to his thighs in water, a hand cupped round each ear.

Mike yelled from the shore. "Joe! What the hell did you drag me down here for?"

Joe shook himself and turned toward Mike.

"Don't just stand there, get out! Your backside is all wet," Mike shouted. "What's Hazel going to say when you get home?"

Hazel. Land woman.

Mike called his name again.

Joe looked far out to sea, where a hand protruded above the

water.

Waving. Saying goodbye.

Judith Field lives in London, UK. She is the daughter of writers, and learned how to agonise over fiction submissions at her mother's (and father's) knee. She's a pharmacist working in emergency medicine, a medical writer, editor, and indexer. She started writing in 2009. She mainly writes speculative fiction, a welcome antidote from the world she lives in. Her work has appeared in a variety of publications in the USA, UK, and Australia. When she's not working or writing, she studies English, knits, sings, and swims, not always at the same time. She blogs at *Luna Station Quarterly*.

This story first appeared in *Stupefying Stories*, March 2014

NOTHING LEFT TO SAY

By Sandy Dee Hall

And so I walk with her down the street. It sounds simple enough, but there is so much to this walk, to these steps. It rains slowly, "not hard enough for an umbrella," she says. But the street is quiet in a way where there is still so much ambient noise but not enough to affect us. There are still the cars driving by, splashing the rain back up to where it came, and there are still the people that walk by huddled in their coats like turtles, and there are still all these things that swirl about us and cocoon us in this blanket of together.

And I walk with her down the street. It sounds simple, but it is hard, because we are not sure how close we can walk, and I am not sure if I can wrap my arm around her smallness and bring her in closer to me to protect her from the rain or the slight wind that picks up now and again, but she bumps into me a few times, and I feel that I can now do it; I can now bring her closer to me where I want her to be.

Now that is accomplished. And we talk.

The last time we spoke for hours in a small wine bar about everything, mostly me I felt but I wanted to know all about her, so I kept trying to ask her as she sat across from me, her yellow eyes reflected in candle light that made her light olive skin glow. The candle danced in her iris as I watched it turn molten and move.

She said back in that wine bar that speaking about the weather was a sign of being uncomfortable with one another and a way to fill the time. Now we walk silently for moments and wait to speak, and she begins by talking about the weather.

I laugh, she laughs and all tension seems to dissolve, because there was tension until that point, but now we walk, and I want to take her small hand in mine, but I won't do that because I don't feel we are "quite there yet" but maybe soon, and the food is good, maybe great, and she eats from my plate and I eat from hers, and I make a little sauce for the bread that comes out of olive oil, pepper, and parmesan cheese.

"I have never had it like this before," she says with her mouth full of bread, and I find it so unbelievably cute and a tad sexy that she will talk while she is eating.

We talk more about life and how the world works or how we think it works. I tell her about how I love fantasy books with elves and magic and such; she laughs at me and tries not to at the same time.

I like that she tries but in truth I am a bit of a dork, and that seems to be okay with her, but I am talking about these things to make a point, because in my favorite book when they speak about moving people, they speak about moving individuals and then those individuals moving others and so on until these drops become ripples and these ripples become waves and these waves create change and that is what I want to do—"I want to change the world"—and this she appreciates, and the laughs stop because I am being serious and she understands. She understands.

I feel that she, who is wrapped in a summer scarf, something I didn't know existed, that she gets me in a some way, and I hope I get her, and I want to know the reason why she reached out to me in that café as I made comments about her reading on a Friday night, which I think is amazing, reading on a Friday night, not drinking and cavorting about town and generally acting like a complete fool, but reading, and I think of that now as I watch her talk about how she understands the need to effect change on an individual level and not just be a cause and become lost in that cause, I think about her curled up in a blanket on some cold night in her old college in Boston and her reading some book that has all of her focus as the fire—yes, there is a fire there—dances on the walls and the world is shut out as the snow fills the streets and the windows fog over, and there she is wrapped in warmth.

We finish dinner and there is a conversation over the bill, as in who should pay, and I insist because, "I asked you to dinner," and she states, "that next time I AM GOING to pay," with a force coating her words that makes me just shake my head and give in.

We walk more. I am distracted by her, by how she walks close to me, because yes, I want to put my arm around her again, so I do, and I am distracted by how she looks directly into my eyes and speaks to me and not at me. I am bringing her to a bakery in the L.E.S. that I want her to try, and she confesses to me that she "might have stalked me a bit before we ever met," and I want to know more about this because this sort of talk intrigues me.

She wraps her arm in mine after she says this as if we have been doing this for years, taking walks in the crisp N.Y. night, quiet after the rain, and beautiful in every street light that illuminates the cracks and window fronts that bring the city to life. She feels good on my arm, warm against my shoulder, and I feel that we could walk like this until the moon has had its say.

I say, "I was going to ask you something but now I am not."

"Why?" she says then adds, "you have to tell me now."

And I do have to tell her now, because once someone says something like that they have to divulge, so I say that I was going to ask for a kiss but I didn't want to make it awkward, and she says, "it is awkward," and we laugh about this.

"I know it is but now I am going to wait," I say.

"I would taste like garlic anyways," she says, and that wouldn't bother me, not in the slightest.

The assumption of it being awkward has not really made it so, but has a left a feeling of expectancy in the air, and now she wonders when will he do it, and I know that she wants me too and I want to as well.

We arrive at the bakery, and of course its closed and of course it is Monday, but it doesn't matter because they let us in because I know them. I go there all the time—four, five times a week—and I have actually spoken to the people in the bakery before about this very girl, about me being nervous and unsure about her company, about how to greet her because we had only communicated in emails until that point—do I give her a kiss on the cheek, a handshake or just a friendly hug, "ass out," the girl at the bakery had said as they practiced all these different greetings in front of me, putting a show for my view.

The people at the bakery offer us any of the items that lie strewn across the counter, mostly breads, but I hold them up for Erica—that's her name—but she doesn't look like an Erica, not really, because she is much more exotic than that, but Erica is a great name, and when I look at her again I think that maybe she is an Erica.

She chooses the chocolate chip banana bread over the plain banana and some other forgotten type because, "why would you choose plain banana when you can get it with chocolate chips," and this reasoning is flawless, perfectly logical.

We talk with the bakers some and then are removed from the premises because they want to leave as well. We sit on a stoop out front, and the street is surprisingly busy for a Monday and the light is soft.

Another group of people try to get into the closed bakery after we exit. We giggle at them as they are rejected by the staff, and as they walk, away I say, "aren't you impressed that they let us in now?"

"Yes, I am," she says.

We eat the extremely moist and overly delicious chocolate chip banana loaf and begin to talk about words, words like moist because I say, "moist really does sound like it is said," and we begin to talk about strange words, or other words that sound like they are spoken, and she says, "I had a whole list of those types of words," and I am surprised by this and ask her what these words are, and she says, "I can't think of any right now."

"Why can't you?"

"Because I am distracted," and she looks quickly up at me and back down at the bread in her hands and I know that it is right now, that I have to do it or forego ever doing it again.

Our legs touch from hip to thigh we sit pushed together on the red steps. I smile at her and take her by her chin and say very softly, a whisper in the wind, "come here."

She turns her head to me slowly and we close our eyes on that stoop and shut out everything but this. Our lips meet and hers are soft and giving, and the sounds from around us cease, no honks or shouts break through our bubble, and I reach up and touch her face slightly and slip my hand toward the back of her head. We kiss for a minute or seven but probably just a few seconds and pull apart slowly, slightly remiss, our lips sticking together from the remnants of agave that still sweeten our mouths.

Her face lingers near mine and when I open my eyes I see that she is smiling ever so slightly.

I smile back.

We are quiet for a while as the noises and lights of the city come back to us, not in a flurry but a slow increase as if someone is slowly dialing up the volume on some speaker somewhere. I sit content knowing that it was worth the wait. We finish our pieces of bread and she takes one home to give to her roommate, but I hope she simply eats it on the train on the way home.

I walk her to the train, our night now complete. The walk back is a slow pace taking in the sights of the L.E.S. which are all storefronts and so many salons—four on each block—and cafés and music venues.

We say nothing now, nothing more needing to be said, just arms entwined as we get closer to the uptown 6 train that she will leave me to go home on. We stand in front of the stairs, and I wonder when I will see her again; it seems like a long time from now, days, weeks when I would prefer minutes or hours, "but," she says, "we will talk."

And with that, she reaches up with her small hand and pulls my head down to hers and kisses me just so on the mouth, once, twice; her hand leaves my face. "Bye," she says as she flits out of my line of sight and down the stairs to get her subway.

I walk across the street at a jog, trying to out step the past two hours, to wrap my head around what all just transpired, wrap my head around her and what it all means, because what does it all mean, these little collisions in time?

I know that right now I am happy, content with everything around me and I think that is enough. It is enough.

———

Sandy Dee Hall is a chef from NYC. He now works for his non-profit Sourc.ed. A non-profit for change of food and its access to youth. Don't get lost out there!

DEACTIVATE ME AT WOUNDED KNEE

By Maureen Bowden

Date: July 30, 1895.

Location: London, England.

Professor Barnaby Wolstencraft was a genius, but he was mad. He wore a US cavalry uniform with a wide-brimmed black hat, and his grey hair, dyed bottle blonde, hung in ringlets to his shoulders.

The professor tinkered with his latest invention, the mandrone duplicator, while his assistant, Arthur Bessant, who was also a genius but not mad, painted the time machine. It resembled a steam engine cabin, with space for a driver, a passenger, and a limited amount of equipment they might consider essential. The control panel contained only a destination unit and a starter lever designed to spring back into the "off" position when the machine reached its destination.

Arthur admired his handiwork. The cabin was as green as riverside moss, and gold scrollwork above the door read, "The Lucy Bessant." He squinted in the mid-day sun that blazed through the laboratory's high window, bemoaned the lack of ventilation, and called to the professor, "Why don't you take off your hat, Prof? It's hot in here."

The professor put down his screwdriver and wiped the sweat out of his eyes with an oil-stained, spotted handkerchief. "General George Armstrong Custer wore this hat at the Battle of the Little Bighorn. He was a great man, and I wear it in his memory, hot or not."

Arthur considered the Great George to have been a narcissistic, murderous megalomaniac, but he kept his opinion to himself. The

137

prof was unpredictable. It wasn't wise to agitate him. "How did you get it?"

"I went on a pilgrimage to Montana in '77, the year after the battle, and I won it in a poker game." Arthur wondered how many of "Custer's hats" had been won or lost in poker games since then.

The duplicator's hum rose to a higher pitch. It shuddered, and then fell silent. Arthur dropped his paintbrush and ran to the contraption he called the glass coffin. "Are the mandrones cooked, Prof?"

"Let's find out, shall we?" the prof asked. "I'll materialise the first one." He took a metal pin, on the end of a wire, attached to the duplicator control box, and inserted it into a slot on the side of the coffin. A humanoid figure appeared behind the glass panel. The prof opened the door. "Step out," he said.

The figure obeyed. It wore a US cavalry uniform with a wide-brimmed black hat; its blonde hair hung in ringlets to its shoulders; it held a rifle in one hand and a revolver in the other. Its eyes reminded Arthur of the porcelain doll his daughter, Lucy, insisted on taking to bed. Their lack of humanity made him shiver. Were Custer's eyes like that?

"How many of them are ready to be materialised?" Arthur asked.

"Three thousand. I shall call this one George the First. I've programmed him to command the other two-thousand-nine hundred-and-ninety-nine, and I've programmed them to obey him." He produced a bottle of sherry and two glasses from the recesses of his desk. "Time to celebrate, my boy. I'm taking three thousand General Custers back to the Little Bighorn to help the original Custer win the battle." He poured the sherry, passed a glass to Arthur, and raised the other in a toast. "To the regiment."

Arthur drank, although he felt sick with apprehension. He regretted participating in the creation of something monstrous, and guilt weighed heavily upon him. "I know you admire Custer, Prof," he said, "but do you really think the Sioux wars were justified? Look what happened at Wounded Knee in 1890."

The prof shrugged. "If we win at the Little Bighorn, Wounded Knee won't be necessary."

Arthur had his doubts about the prof's logic, but he knew it was pointless to argue with a fanatic. "When are you leaving?"

"Tomorrow."

When they locked the laboratory that evening, Arthur slipped the spare key into his waistcoat pocket. He wished the prof good night, and walked through Regent's Park gates, as if taking his customary short cut home. After waiting until he was sure the prof was some distance away, he retraced his steps back to the laboratory and let himself in. George the First stood to attention and saluted. Arthur returned the salute. "At ease, General. Turn around. I need to modify your programme."

George the First obeyed, and Arthur pressed the silver deactivating disc located between the mandrone's shoulder blades. George the First slept. Arthur lifted a flap on the back of the mandrone's head, hidden by his ringlets, and removed the mechanical brain. He tapped a selection of numbered keys, inserting the mathematical formula for justice and compassion. After re-installing the brain, Arthur closed the flap, reactivated the mandrone by pressing the silver disc again, and said, "Thank you. Carry on, General." George the First carried on standing at attention. Arthur looked into his eyes, hoping to detect a change. He thought he saw an expression of curiosity, or at least doubt. It would have to be enough.

He climbed into the time machine and opened the destination unit. It was set for June 25, 1876, the banks of the Little Bighorn River, Eastern Montana: the date and place of Custer's last stand. "Please forgive me, prof," he said to himself. "I can't let you interfere with history. Who knows what the consequences would be?" He changed the time setting to a thousand years in the future. By then, he thought, scientists should be advanced enough to find a harmless occupation for a mad genius and three thousand metal humanoids.

On a whim, he changed the named destination to Wounded Knee Creek, Pine Ridge, South Dakota. He couldn't explain why, but his instinct told him it was the right thing to do. Finally, he added a self-destruct command to the destination unit, set to activate when the journey was complete. The machine would be going nowhere else. History would be safe from interference. He locked the laboratory and walked home. The setting sun stained the clouds pink, the evening air was cool, and life was good.

That night, Arthur slept easier than he had since he and the prof built the time machine and began designing mandrones.

Next morning, they loaded the duplicator control box and the glass coffin into "The Lucy Bessant." There was barely enough room left for the prof and George the First. "I'm sorry I can't take you too, Arthur," the prof said. "Maybe next time."

"Of course, Prof. Maybe next time."

The prof pulled back the starter lever. The machine whined, clanged, and vanished. Professor Barnaby Wolstencraft, his time machine, and his mandrone headed for the future.

Arthur turned his attention to designing and manufacturing clockwork toys that Lucy loved, and that someday would make him a rich man.

Date: October 31, 2207.

Location: Pine Ridge Reservation, South Dakota, North America.

Broken Shell, a Holy Woman of the Oglala Sioux, sat cross-legged, facing her fire. She cast a handful of herbs into the flames, inhaled the fumes, and left her body. She called to the Holy Men and Women of the Tribes throughout Dakota, Arizona, Utah, and the rest of the continent.

They responded, "We hear you, Broken Shell."

The Holy Woman spoke. "The Burning Ground, that the Wasichu call Yellowstone, will awaken and roar before the next full moon. It will vomit fire from the earth's belly; ash will fall and darken the sky. The shoreline's bones will shake, and the seas will invade the land."

"What must we do, Broken Shell?"

"Lead your people to the Sacred Mountains. The Great Spirit will protect them until the Burning Ground sleeps again. Bring animals with you. They will breed, and provide food and clothing for our children and their children and all generations to come."

The Tribes travelled to the Black Hills. They sang to the Great Spirit. The sound of their voices formed a dome that protected them from the mighty volcano's fire, and the anger of the earth and sea.

Death took all who were not protected, and when the Burning Ground slept again, the Tribes reclaimed the land that had been theirs before the Wasichu came, and they honoured it. The land nurtured them, and the Tribes prospered.

Date: Two moons after the Spring Equinox, 2895.

Location: South Dakota plains, North America.

The time machine materialised on the outskirts of the prosperous Pine Ridge rural settlement, in a peaceful land. George the First helped Professor Barnaby Wolstencraft out of the cabin.

The professor looked around. "This doesn't look like Montana. George, see if you can locate the battleground while I set up the duplicator. Arm yourself in case you run into any renegade Redskins."

George the First marched toward Pine Ridge with his rifle on his shoulder. Before he reached the settlement, he encountered a young Redskin woman sitting alone in the shade of a tree. His flora and fauna education programme enabled him to identify it as a pine.

"General Custer, I presume," she said. "I've been expecting you."

"Why? Who are you?"

"Falling Cone, descendant of the Oglala Sioux Holy Woman, Broken Shell. She foretold your return. Since the Burning Ground changed this land, each generation has passed her words down to me."

"Were your ancestor's words a warning?"

"Yes. I must help you to solve a puzzle. If I fail, my people will die by your hand." She patted the ground. "Sit."

"I have no time. I must find the battleground."

"You're a little late. Sit."

Since Arthur's modification, George the First had been aware of unease in his brain, where before, there had been only certainty. Maybe this woman, who he felt compelled to obey, would have the solution. He sat.

Falling Cone said, "I can tell by your eyes that you're an android. My people have no use for such things, but in other lands they're used as servants, love toys, or weapons. Let me guess. You're a weapon."

"I am, but the word 'android' is not in my vocabulary store. My maker calls me a mandrone."

"A metal man by any other name ... What's the puzzle?"

He told her of his maker, Professor Barnaby Wolstencraft; the two-thousand-nine-hundred-and-ninety-nine George Armstrong Custers under his command; and the plan to win the Battle of the Little Bighorn. "My maker called me George the First and I knew my purpose, until his assistant, who was called Arthur, modified my programme."

"Arthur set you the puzzle?"

"Yes. He made me unsure of what command I should give. Can you help me?"

"You can help yourself. Arthur became your maker. Obey him. Your true name is Arthur the Second."

"Thank you. I believe Arthur's intention was that I should not fight the Battle of the Little Bighorn, but the professor will not agree. Custer is his hero. He wears his hat."

"It doesn't matter a coyote's fart whether he agrees or not. Custer lost his hat more than a thousand years ago, and you're in South Dakota, not Montana."

"I will try to make him understand."

Arthur the Second returned to the time machine, where the professor and two-thousand-nine-hundred-and-ninety-nine General Custers were waiting for him. "We are in the wrong time and the wrong place," he said. "The battle was lost long ago."

The professor didn't appear to hear him. "Did you come across any Redskins?"

"Yes. We are close to a settlement of the Sioux Tribe."

"Then do your duty, General. They must be destroyed, or this land will never be at peace."

"This land is at peace, Professor. The wars are over."

"Do as I command. You are a mandrone, and I am your maker."

A plan was forming in Arthur the Second's mind. He led the regiment of mandrones away from the mad professor. The Tribe emerged from the settlement to protect their families. They carried only farming implements as weapons, which were no defence against rifles and revolvers.

Arthur the Second ordered the mandrones to form a circle. They obeyed. He ordered them to turn left, so that they were each facing the back of another mandrone. They obeyed. He ordered them to press the silver disc between the mandrones' shoulders. They obeyed. Two-thousand-nine-hundred-and-ninety-nine General Custers dropped their weapons and slept.

Professor Barnaby Wolstencraft's wail echoed across the plains. "No! What have you done?" He knelt beside his fallen regiment and picked up a rifle. "Cowards. You're all cowards. I'll kill them myself," he yelled, running toward the unarmed Sioux. Arthur the Second aimed his own rifle and blew the back off the professor's head.

He carried him back to the "The Lucy Bessant." The Tribe followed in silence. He placed the body in the glass coffin and began to dig a grave with his bare hands. A man of the Tribe tapped his shoulder and handed him a spade. "This will save your finger nails and take less time."

He buried the mad genius in the coffin, along with the duplicator control box, and then he helped the Tribe to pile the mandrones into a high mound with "The Lucy Bessant" beneath it. The passing of time would rust and disintegrate the metal, the synthetic skin and fabric would turn to dust, and the mound would be scattered by the prairie wind.

The Tribe returned to their settlement. Arthur the Second stood alone on the Dakota plains and wished for annihilation. He sought out Falling Cone. "My purpose is fulfilled," he said. "I ask you to deactivate me. Press the silver disc on my back and I will sleep."

"You saved my people. We thank you."

"You should thank Arthur. I obeyed his orders."

"We honour the splinter of Arthur's spirit that he passed to you, and we'll honour your remains." She pressed the silver disc between his shoulder blades and Arthur the Second slept. Falling Cone placed her hand upon his head. "I know nothing of the land to which an android's soul must travel, or who will be waiting to welcome you, but I wish you a swift journey. May you find peace."

The Elders of the Tribe carried the mandrone's body high into the Black Hills. In the cool mountain air, they laid it on a flat boulder and covered it with rocks to protect it from tornados, hailstorms, and the South Dakota sun.

Maureen Bowden is a Liverpudlian living with her musician husband in North Wales. She has had over a hundred stories and poems accepted for publication by paying markets. Silver Pen publishers nominated one of her stories for the 2015 international Pushcart Prize. She also writes song lyrics, mostly comic political satire, set to traditional melodies. Her husband has performed these in Folk clubs throughout England and Wales. She loves her family and friends, Rock 'n' Roll, Shakespeare, and cats.

RESOURCES

SCENES AROUND THE LAB
By Lady C. Zytal, as provided by Lucinda Gunnin

Hello darlings—

When last we chatted, I told you about my beautiful pre-historic plant, ridding my garden of pesky squirrels and other vermin. I thought we were well on our way to spring, and I'd be able to enjoy the pale orange blossoms for months to come.

Unfortunately, my lovely *Amelia* didn't make it through this dastardly spring. I think I've heard reference made to the third or possibly fourth winter we're having this year, and to be quite frank, I'm over it. Snow flurries in mid-April, days after seeing 85 degrees and sunshine, will ruin this girl's mood and kill a perfectly harmless carnivorous, invasive species.

I was so devastated by the loss of my gorgeous *Amelia* that I paid the gardener for overtime and leapt aboard the *Americana* to see if I could find spring somewhere else in history.

Since we've all heard that Paris is lovely in the spring, my beleaguered Captain Sven took us to Paris in 1895. While enjoying lunch near the university, I happened to encounter Maria Sklodwska, whom most of you know as Marie Curie. Okay, fine, it wasn't happenstance. I may have sought her out. It was Women's History Month, and I wondered if Marie had any idea how much influence she would have on women in the future.

Imagine my surprise what Marie told me a strange tale that indicated she knew exactly where her future would lead her. History tells us that Maria was the fifth and youngest child of school teachers in what would become Poland, but I found out that was a carefully crafted alternative fact (a lie, darlings!).

147

Maria and Pierre actually hailed from the 22nd century and ended up in France through a series of experiments gone slightly awry. Maria, whom everyone in France called Marie, was a young physicist in the domed city of Berlin in 2187 working on time travel when she met Pierre, an older visiting scientist from the South American continent and living primarily in the domed city of São Paulo.

While Pierre was visiting, Maria perfected the light stabilization core necessary to create her time portals. Unfortunately, in her exhaustion from a late night of discussing theoretical worm holes with Pierre and teaching her 6 a.m. introductory physics classes, Maria neglected to lock up the remote control for the time portal. To no one's surprise, her most advanced and mischievous students, Paulette and Bruner, borrowed the device and travelled back in time. Their destination? Paris, mid-1880s.

Paulette later told Maria they had chosen the era because they had hoped to see an unspoiled forest outside of a dome and perhaps peek at the ocean before it became filled with toxic sludge. They'd been gone about three hours when Maria discovered the theft. Her dilemma was that reporting the theft meant the students would be expelled from their studies, despite being brilliant, and that the remote only held the portal open for 16 hours. She hoped to extend the battery life in the future, but that was never to be.

Since Pierre was a visiting professor and not part of the administration, and someone she could trust, Maria told him of the issue. His affection for Marie already blooming, Pierre volunteered to go fetch the students back, knowing Maria would be missed if she did not make it to her evening teaching assignments.

He was gone about four hours when Maria found the second problem with her device. Each person who used the portal incrementally decreased the life of the battery. Risking her own position at the university, Maria jumped through the portal, hoping to return Pierre to his rightful time line.

But it was not to be. By the time they recovered the errant students, the portal's light had faded to a dim blue.

"Marie told me that there was only enough battery life left for two people to make it back to our home," Pierre told me as we walked along the Seine. "I didn't want to go back without her and she was too devoted to her students to go without them."

In the end, the students were able to make it home and send through enough historical data that Marie and Pierre could invent their own histories.

"We considered replicating the time portals from here," Maria told me, "but we were afraid that it might speed up the destruction of the planet. In fact, no one was supposed to know about my experiments, but one of our colleagues was so excited by them he told an administrator, and suddenly the university was thinking money-making opportunities."

Marie intends to downplay her discoveries during this lifetime but create a framework for physicists in the future.

After her fascinating, but unbelievable story, I asked Maria about their wedding plans. I fainted when she told me she intended to get married in the blue suit she usually wore to the lab.

I awoke aboard the *Americana*, where Sven insisted I had developed a poor reaction to the local wine and needed immediate medical treatment. My feverish ramblings about Pierre and Marie Curie concerned the crew, he said, so we needed to find a doctor capable of more "than applying leeches."

I certainly wasn't down for leeches, but I did wonder how much of Maria's tale was true. Were they just jesting with a slightly tipsy time traveler?

The shipboard doctor, who is really more of a time paramedic, gave me a hot toddy to ward off the cold-like symptoms, some Vitamin C, and a couple anti-radiation tablets, since we now know Marie wasn't exactly practicing safety precautions in her lab.

What happened next could have been because of my delirium, as Sven claimed, or it could mean we have a bit more trouble with the *Americana's* time drive that I previously anticipated.

Sven still claims that not five minutes after receiving my dosing from the doc, I came into the ship's command center and demanded to be allowed to play with the time drive setting. Sven says I claimed I knew exactly the right doctor for my ailment and proceeded to twist knobs and push buttons that explicitly say, "Do not touch."

That really doesn't sound like me. I think the ship malfunctioned.

Regardless of how it happened, we bopped through a time jump only to find ourselves over a turbulent sea in an unknown place where cities rose on platforms above the brine. Sven and I were so captivated with the landscape that we almost missed the approach of the privateers in an airship looked to be held together with duct tape and chewing gum.

In a moment of lucidity, I managed to flip the switch for the *Americana's* internal cloaking system, which instantly transformed Sven and his pistol to an orphan with a mop and bucket and me into some old school marm, running a crew of drunks and orphans.

The Silent Monsoon came alongside our port and sent out the boarding planks. It didn't take an engineer to see that the old ship, though well-tended and loved, was in rough shape. Capt. Svetlana Tereshchenko assured me as she came aboard that they meant us no harm, but that they were inspecting all cargo ships on behalf of the regional port authority, trying to find a missing cask of something or other.

Her story was nonsense and I knew it, just as she knew with a glance that Sven and the others were no orphans.

"Nice cloaking device. Mine can't do people or the ship's interior," she said, letting me know that what I thought I saw of *The Silent Monsoon* was as much an illusion as Sven's mop.

Svetlana is a crusty ol' girl, so I didn't ask what became of her eye. Instead, we shared a discussion of trade routes over a cup of tea and Tim Tams. When Svetlana was convinced we didn't have her missing cask, I offered her a few extra barrels of rations that we keep aboard for just such events. It's salted pork and dried beef that Chef Angela would die before preparing, but it's good for giving away as good will.

I thanked her kindly for her guide to Heliopolis, and the ships parted ways. It wasn't until a week later that I noticed the voice crank box missing from my curios shelf. The small device is perfect for those parties when I haven't managed an invitation or when I need to go undercover to get the story. A brass contraption similar to the inner workings of a music box, with fine tuning the voice crank box can imitate almost any voice with uncanny accuracy. I supposed there's no reason Svetlana can't borrow it until I need it again.

Upon returning to the current timeline, I was devastated to find that Princess Tartan had not, in fact, kidnapped the world leader as previously indicated. The princess told me privately that she had to rewind time and put him back at her father's insistence.

The Junoian king said the removal would cause too much upheaval on Earth and that "Americans haven't learned their lesson yet. We'll see if they figure it out soon."

So, as I lament a late spring, a kidnapping that never happened, and a theft that happened right before my eyes, I'm heading to the shore house. If it's not warm enough to open the doors and enjoy some sunshine, I'm headed south of the equator, as this never-ending cycle of wet and cold has left me in need of rum, beach, and sun.

TTFN,

Lady C.

———

Lady C. Zytal was born just off the Main Line in Pennsylvania when such a thing still mattered, the first daughter of a family whom she prefers not to name. She makes her home aboard the airship *Americana*, when not at her summer lair in the Canadian Rockies or wintering on a private island near the Bahamas. Zytal considers Liz Smith her most apt pupil and the best mentor she ever had. She's also been known to denigrate simpleton scientists whose creativity ends at a bloody lab coat and death ray.

———

Lucinda Gunnin lives just west of the Main Line. She's lived in the Philly suburbs long enough to love cheesesteaks, fear scrapple and think that Amish smorgasbords are generally overrated.

She still isn't sure she pronounces or spells Schuylkill right and hasn't gotten used to bridges that are two centuries old. She loves non-grape fruit wines, all-you-can-eat sushi, gaming of all types and her very spoiled cat. She writes whatever catches her fancy this week, and has published poetry, science fiction and other short stories, and romance novellas.

YOU "OORT" TO KNOW

Advice by Dr. Arthur "Oort" Cloud,
as provided by Sean Frost
With questions provided by Tim McDaniel (Dr. Clive
Crawley), Pol Jackson (Unsigned), and Dawn Vogel
(H'wr2uoia 17)

———————

Dear Mad Scientist Journal,

You must understand, I must first state, that I rarely seek assistance, relief, from others. When I was at the Institute I did, indeed, occasionally work with assistants—yes, mere assistants—and in every case they betrayed me, deceived me, double-crossed me—it was Helman—yes, Helman!—who purloined my plans for the non-stick lampshade, Denavov who stole my magnetic crabapples! And who, I ask you—who took that last donut, or perhaps doughnut (if Swenson is to be believed, the vile worm!), from the break room on that fateful, ill-fated Saturday? Knaves and fools, all of them! They could not understand, could not comprehend! Mere pretenders to greatness! Thieves and laughing jackanapes! Maybe even jackalopes, at times! It is possible, yes, even likely! But I will show them all, I tell you!

Nevertheless, I am not one to hold a grudge, to harbor antipathy. No! When my enemies are made to suffer my wrath, I will rest content, I will no longer feel the burn or suffer their laughter. So I ask you: I had a cat, yes, I believe it was a cat, without eyestalks, which I had injected with certain chemical compounds. And why not? I had the cat, I had the chemicals! Then there was a gamma-ray generator. My question, my query: how does one get the smell out of the drapery? It is intolerable—unendurable, I tell you! I will have an answer!

Cordially yours,
Dr. Clive Crawley

Dear Dr. Crawley,

If I understand the thrust of your query—and allow me to say that I by no means place the burden of any misapprehension at your feet, or indeed at whatever appendages you may have, not wanting to assume anything about your physical nature for the sake of a rhetorical device; it is so important in our modern age to be cognizant of the linguistic bias in our discourse that may serve to reinforce cultural prejudices of bygone eras that may be hurtful to those members of traditionally repressed groups on whose ears our words may fall.

If, as I was saying, I have properly gleaned the intent of your letter, it seems that in the course conducting a perfectly reasonable experiment upon a cat, involving certain chemicals and gamma radiation, an odor has settled into your curtains. As a caution for my other readers, this is not an entirely unprecedented occurrence. I myself went through several furnishings before confining my work to stainless steel laboratories. It is simply untenable to keep replacing household items that were never meant to withstand the conditions at the rough edge of science.

Replacement is what's required, I'm sorry to say. In my experience, that odor will never come out. I've tried every spray and laundry soap on the market (as well as several that are not available to the general public), and nothing removes that incredible stench.

I do hope the cat is well. They are such versatile animals, being especially suited for genetic modification.

Yours in Science!
Dr. Oort

~

What is the guiltiest element?

Dear Writer,
I usually decline the more philosophical questions. The esoteric

is fine for research topics, but until successful results are published, it's all just theory. That's not to say that there are no intriguing avenues of exploration. In fact, for matters of the soul alone there are dozens of battered journals and survivor accounts that can set you on your path.

My reluctance has more to do with the letters that I get whenever I tackle these questions. There's nothing like laying out theories about the unsolved to bring out the angry and certain correspondents!

Nevertheless, I was compelled to share this question for its meditative value. Like a zen koan, its very insolubility puts into doubt the very concept of searching for truth. Guilt is both a human emotional concept and a declaration of responsibility. What do either have to do with elements, either scientific or alchemical? It's fodder for a lot of fruitless thought and speculation.

That said, since the letters will come anyway, I'll put my money down on carbon.

Yours in Science!

Dr. Oort

~

Dear Mad Scientist,

It seems inevitable that in every mad scientist's career, they must make use of a "lair" in an unpopulated part of the world. Unfortunately, the only unpopulated portions of my world are blisteringly cold, and no one lives there because we simply cannot. I would love advice on how to make things work in an inhospitable climate, or, failing that, the best methods of mass depopulation of an inhabitable region.

Yours,

H'wr2uoia 17

Dear 17,

As scientists on or even beyond the fringes of accepted practice, it is often necessary to secret our operations in the remote, inaccessible, and unpopulated regions of the world. This is a hardship not only because of the outlandish shipping charges, but due to the extra barrier of entry to the field. To wit, one must be a master of building laboratory and living quarters for extreme environments! Why, from my graduating class alone, nearly 37% of those pursuing careers in alternative science perished from inferior venting in a volcano hideout before our 5-year reunion! (His name was Edmund. A delightful fellow, but a touch inattentive to details.)

Luckily, you now have options—that is, if your bank account has enough zeroes in the right places. A cottage industry has cropped up to provide dedicated researchers with fully functional facilities, or "lairs" as you so colorfully put it. Traditional options are available: volcanic islands, mountaintop keeps, even underground habitations with mole people for manual labor. There are also new designs for the modern urbanite. How would you like to work in your own skyscraper? Or perhaps you prefer the blight esthetic of an abandoned factory.

Whatever your preference, there are companies to cater to your needs. Building your new headquarters has never been safer or easier. It's raising the capital to fund it that's the real problem.

Yours in Science!

Dr. Oort

———

Dr. Oort has PhDs in Astrophysics, Mathematics, Linguistics, and Paleobiology; a MA in Philosophy; MSs in Computer Science, Mechanical Engineering, Electrical Engineering, Chemistry, Botany, and Biology; and a BA in Communication. He has written several books that explain the principles of accepted science to those practicing on the fringe, including the best-sellers *Is It?*, *It Is*, and *What Is It Now?* When not giving talks on alternative paths to Truth, Dr. Cloud continues his efforts to breed the perfect lab rat.

———

Sean Frost is a software developer in Michigan, who writes comics and stories while watching horror and science fiction movies. He lives with four demanding cats and a very understanding wife. It is entirely likely that he has a few too many hobbies.

———

Tim McDaniel teaches English as a Second Language at Green River College, not far from Seattle. His short stories, mostly comedic, have appeared in a number of SF/F magazines, including *F&SF*, *Analog*, and *Asimov's*. He lives with his wife, dog, and cat, and his collection of plastic dinosaurs is the envy of all who encounter it. Check out his author page on Amazon.

Pôl Jackson is the spitting image of Mad King Ludwig. He likes tea, cats, temporal paradoxes, and beating imaginary people up.

Dawn Vogel writes and edits both fiction and non-fiction. Her academic background is in history, so it's not surprising that much of her fiction is set in earlier times. By day, she edits reports for historians and archaeologists. In her alleged spare time, she runs a craft business, co-edits *Mad Scientist Journal*, and tries to find time for writing. She is a member of Broad Universe, SFWA, and Codex Writers. Her steampunk series, *Brass and Glass*, is being published by Razorgirl Press. She lives in Seattle with her awesome husband (and fellow author), Jeremy Zimmerman, and their herd of cats. Visit her at historythatneverwas.com

CLASSIFIEDS

Education

EVIL GENIUS TRAINING: Are you overwhelmingly ambitious, systematically villainous, or dangerously ambivalent about which lines should never be crossed? Apply now to the Evil Genius Vocational College! By the end of our 12-week course, you'll be propping your entire life up with hubris, playing god with absolutely no hesitation, and using new technologies to hold the world ransom—and all before lunchtime! Call now 555-3845.

—Tom Lund

For Rent—Laboratory Space

PROPERTY FOR RENT: 1,100 sq ft research facility with attached living quarters and 2-cell subterranean dungeon (outside access only). Property has been completely renovated and is ready for a new occupant. Applicants must agree to 2-year lease and pass a credit check. Don't worry, no background check required! $850/mo.

—Tom Lund

For Sale—Equipment

Dynatech Unveils Self-Installers: Be More than Yourself, without the Doctor Fees!

Stop moving and shut up, because Dynatech has new tech that you're going to want to buy, ASAP.

Fresh from the minds of our country's greatest researchers, with development personally overseen by Arcuis Elmwood himself, comes the newest upgrade to Dynatech's already flawless, revolutionary cybernetics: self-installation!

Cut out the middle man, and cut out the crap! Stop worrying about exorbitant hospital fees. Why give money to some so-called doctors, when you can thank the creators of your newest body modification with pure profits?

—Kevin Holton

For Sale—Pets

FOR SALE: Slightly used Igor. House trained and capable of some menial tasks, but has been known to eat lab rats. Suffers from mild amnesia due to his recent overdose on neurotoxins. Will work for room and board or a sufficient supply of lab rats. He prefers the pink ones. Price negotiable. Call Tessa at 555-555-5555.

—Lucinda Gunnin

For sale: seven hoo-men and seven woo-men (which is what they call themselves, so yeah, we're just as confused as you) from an undisclosed planet. Captured onboard a vessel on the dark side of the Traca moon, these specimens seem to belong to an ancient culture that is either undiscovered or no longer exists. They're a clever kind, with the capacity to build little huts from pretty much any tools. They come in a variety of colors. Available for individual purchase or in pairs. Warning, very violent and very physically active. If you do not plan to breed them, we suggest having them fixed.

—Joachim Heijndermans

We offer twenty adorable rescue kittens who are in need of a new home. They were rescued from an illegal kickstart lab in São Paolo, found malnourished and neglected. These little critters just need a little TLC and they'll be the perfect pets. The kittens (four European short hairs, two Persians, seven lynxes and seven smilodons) can be excellent companions when given the right home. So please call SavCat to learn more.

(Note: smilodon kittens grow up quick, so please make sure you can afford their distinct diet of mammoth meat and have plenty of room for them to play. SavCat is not responsible for any damages or injuries sustained from adopted animals).

—Joachim Heijndermans

Help Wanted

HELP WANTED: Airship pilot and navigator. Must be comfortable at formal gatherings and society events. Ability to navigate time travel is expected, but fascination with said travel is not. Compensation including lodging and meals aboard the Americana, entrance to high society functions around the mad science world, and a nominal salary. Wardrobe allowance may be included as part of an optional side hustle as arm candy for a world-renowned reporter. Preference given to persons with tattoos, visible piercings, or other distinctive and interesting personalities or foibles. Contact ladyczytal@madsciencereports.com.

—Lucinda Gunnin

HELP WANTED: Party planner for upcoming May Day celebration. Decorations must include comfortable surfaces, preferably in velvet or other soft textures, as traditional May Day apparel is expected. Experience with a may pole and the accompanying rites is preferred. Absolutely no roses or other thorny vegetation may be part of the garden party decorations. Adequate protection for burns from garden warming stations will be appreciated. Applicants should include a digital portfolio from previous events and the dates and times of those events, as I prefer to see them for myself before making a decision. Contact: ladyczytal@mainlinenakedgardening.com

—Lucinda Gunnin

WANTED: Knight for hire. Must be brave, must have seen battle before, must be able to successfully slay dragon. In addition to this, applicant must understand that he will not be marrying the princess of this kingdom, as she is already spoken for, and also must realize that any medical damages he may accrue during battle are to be paid for on his own, should he decide to give up during battle and live to tell the tale. However, all successful applicants will be given a sum of no less than 100,000,000 gold coins along with the hand of any of the princess' maids in waiting that he should choose.

—Linda M. Crate

HELP WANTED: Lab Assistant. Filling recent vacancy in alchemical laboratory. Seeking driven self-starter to assist in conducting experiments and observing results in a less-than-controlled environment. The ideal applicant will have at 3 years' experience handling dragons. Fast reflexes are a plus. Resistance to fire preferred, but not required.

—Tom Lund

Lost Items

Missing: 7th Universe. Have you seen our Universe? It is the 7th Universe of the Infinite Continuum, left of the dark Abyss and right of the slightly brighter Abyss that has that funky color scheme. We can't seem to find it, and we've double checked, so no, we didn't misplace it. It contains all our worlds, stars, nebulas, roads, houses, and movie stars (there are some jerks, which we can live without, but we'll take them if it means retrieving our Universe). We really want it back, so if you've seen it, please contact us. We're currently rooming with our friends Suliotharn and Janet, and you can contact us there (they said they're in the book, whatever that means).

We are willing to offer a reward for our Universe. Right now we can only offer six-million gold[2], but once we get our Universe back, we can offer you more (we have year passes to our version of Terra Kewl Park, which come with a drink, a stay at the hotel, and Terragator attack insurance). So please, if you know more, contact us.

-Idra & Somna Acht, phase shifter agents #0054 and #0155
—Joachim Heijndermans

Lost Pets

LOST: Pet cat. Color and sex unknown. Answers, sometimes, to a shaken box. Contact schroedingerfamilymail@dontlook.com
—Lucinda Gunnin

Lost Pets—Found

Found: one eye of Ganogg, a seven-tentacled beast of the bright Abyss beyond the Amber horizon, where the screams can't be heard and the light shatters. Its skin is red with ebony stripes, while its one eye is an iced blue. Does this little fella belong to you? Name tag reads "Ted". We found it clawing at our sun, trying to consume the light that nurtures our little system. No reward asked or compensation for the stains on our neighbor planets requested.

We just want to get the poor thing back to its rightful home. If "Ted" belongs to you, please contact us ASAP. We noticed him looking expectantly at the rings of our planet.

—Joachim Heijndermans

Personals

PERSONAL: Abigail, I miss you. Hopping through time is dull without you. Text me. –C

—Lucinda Gunnin

Personals—Platonic

Dirty bomb looking for a friend: Hi. My name is Stewart. I'm a short distance tactical nuclear missile. My designated number is: 34779123, and I'm looking for a friend. As a weapon of mass destruction whose production type has been halted, it's hard to make connections. My life has gotten very lonely, especially after the last war used up most of my remaining friends. I mostly sit around in my silo, keeping myself busy. But the loneliness has gotten to be too much for me, so I wanted to reach out for some companionship.

My hobbies include math, chess, radiology, sudoku, aerodynamics and making amusing anagrams. I also like to watch reruns of "Laverne and Shirley" and "Cheers" (before Diane left). I'm anxious to meet people, so please drop a line at 34779123@hogomail.gov. Looking forward to chatting.

-Stewart

—Joachim Heijndermans

ABOUT

BIOS FOR CLASSIFIEDS AUTHORS

Linda M. Crate is a Pennsylvanian native born in Pittsburgh yet raised in the rural town of Conneautville. Her poetry, short stories, articles, and reviews have been published in a myriad of magazines both online and in print. She has five published chapbooks *A Mermaid Crashing Into Dawn* (Fowlpox Press - June 2013), *Less Than A Man* (The Camel Saloon - January 2014), *If Tomorrow Never Comes* (Scars Publications, August 2016), *My Wings Were Made to Fly* (Flutter Press, September 2017), and splintered with terror (Scars Publications, January 2018).

~

Lucinda Gunnin lives just west of the Main Line. She's lived in the Philly suburbs long enough to love cheesesteaks, fear scrapple and think that Amish smorgasbords are generally overrated.

She still isn't sure she pronounces or spells Schuylkill right and hasn't gotten used to bridges that are two centuries old. She loves non-grape fruit wines, all-you-can-eat sushi, gaming of all types and her very spoiled cat. She writes whatever catches her fancy this week, and has published poetry, science fiction and other short stories, and romance novellas.

~

Kevin Holton is a cyborg and caffeine addict from coastal New Jersey. He's the author of three forthcoming novels: *The Nightmare King*, *At the Hands of Madness*; and *These Walls Don't Talk, They Scream*. He also co-wrote the short film *Human Report 85616*. His shorter print work has appeared with *Sci-Phi Journal*, *The Literary*

Hatchet, *Radiant Crown Press*, *Pleiades*, *Rain Taxi*, *Mighty Quill Books*, and *Thunderdome Press*, among others. When not reading and writing, he can be found narrating audiobooks, talking about Batman, or recharging in a dark room somewhere.

~

Joachim Heijndermans writes, draws, and paints nearly every waking hour. Originally from the Netherlands, he's been all over the world, boring people by spouting random trivia. His work has been featured in a number of publications, such as *Every Day Fiction*, *Asymmetry Fiction*, and *Gathering Storm Magazine*, and he's currently in the midst of completing his first children's book. You can check out his other work at www.joachimheijndermans.com, or follow him on Twitter: @jheijndermans.

~

From his childhood in the Caribbean to his later years in the Eastern Bloc, Tom has found that sometimes the best way to explore this crazy world is to create your own. He has dabbled in many things, careers and hobbies alike, but has always found that nothing satiates his restless heart more than creating. He currently lives and creates among the red rocks of Southern Utah.

ABOUT THE EDITORS

Dawn Vogel writes and edits both fiction and non-fiction. Her academic background is in history, so it's not surprising that much of her fiction is set in earlier times. By day, she edits reports for historians and archaeologists. In her alleged spare time, she runs a craft business, co-edits *Mad Scientist Journal*, and tries to find time for writing. She is a member of Broad Universe, SFWA, and Codex Writers. Her steampunk series, *Brass and Glass*, is being published by Razorgirl Press. She lives in Seattle with her awesome husband (and fellow author), Jeremy Zimmerman, and their herd of cats. Visit her at historythatneverwas.com.

~

In addition to co-editing *Mad Scientist Journal*, Jeremy Zimmerman is a teller of tales who dislikes cute euphemisms for writing like "teller of tales." He is the author of the young adult superhero book, *Kensei*. Its sequel, *The Love of Danger*, is now available. He lives in Seattle with a herd of cats and his lovely wife (and fellow author) Dawn Vogel. You can learn more about him at bolthy.com.

ABOUT THE ARTIST

Scarlett O'Hairdye is a burlesque performer, producer and artist. To learn more, visit her site at www.scarlettohairdye.com.